UNWELCOME
GUESTS

An atmospheric, suspenseful thriller

ANNA WILLETT

Paperback edition published by

The Book Folks

London, 2018

ISBN 978-1-9836-5366-7

www.thebookfolks.com

For the ones we lost on the way.

Chapter One

"What did you say this guy does?" Caitlin knew she'd already asked, but couldn't remember exactly what Jace had told them. She recalled something vague about security. Looking at the two-storey limestone structure, she wondered how anyone could afford such an impressive house as their holiday home.

"I told you." Jace flung a faded green duffle bag down next to her on the pea gravel driveway. "He runs some big-time security firm. He's got houses all over the place. That's why he said we could use this one. He's hardly ever here." Jace fished a key out of his pocket and dangled it in front of Caitlin's face. "Wait till you see the inside."

Caitlin brushed a strand of auburn hair off her face and glanced over at her husband, Eli. The sunlight picked out a nest of tiny lines around his eyes. Lines born of pain that made her heart ache with loss. He'd been quiet for most of the two-hour drive. She'd hoped a weekend away with Eli's younger brother would be just what he needed. Maybe it would drag him out of the funk he'd been in since they lost the baby, but so far he'd shown little enthusiasm. The miscarriage had been hard on both of

1

them, for a while she'd struggled to get out of bed, but month by month life moved on, carrying her along with it. She just wished Eli could pull himself out of the fog. The distance between them was growing and she didn't have the strength to keep both of them sane.

"What do you think?" She hoped Jace's enthusiasm would infect his brother, but one look at Eli's flat expression told her this was going to be a *long* weekend. *When had he become so self-involved? When did the sorrow they shared become only his?* The urge to get back in the car and have Jace take her home came and then died just as swiftly.

Caitlin looked up at the house's sharply angled rooftop. The sky spread out like an endless dreamscape, pale blue and dotted with wisps of white. *He just needs more time.* So that's what she'd give him.

"I can't get a signal on my phone," Eli spoke for the first time since they pulled off the Highway, his voice flat, disinterested.

"I thought we agreed no phones?" Caitlin tried to make her words sound playful, but resentment stewed in the pit of her stomach.

Eli dragged his eyes away from the screen. "I know but we need to have the option." He held her gaze. "For emergencies."

"Relax." Jace stood at the front door. "You can survive without a phone line or Wi-Fi for two days. It's only a thirty-minute drive to Mandurah, it's not like we're in the middle of the Amazon."

Caitlin held her breath and waited for Eli to argue. Instead, he nodded and for the first time that day a smile softened his lips. She hated to think of herself as a nag, but talking him into accepting Jace's invitation had been a good move. Jace always knew how to handle his older brother.

"Okay, enough standing around." Jace jingled the key again and then slid it into the lock. "Time for the tour."

The oversized wooden door swung inwards reminding her of entering a church; Caitlin hesitated before following Jace inside.

"It's incredible, isn't it?" He turned and walked backwards into a sitting room, his voice bouncing off the stone floor and high ceilings.

They followed Jace through the cavernous lounge where a reclaimed tree trunk, knobbly and highly polished, stood from floor to ceiling. In front of the beam a large, raw-brick, dome fireplace with an inky-black flue darted up the length of the tree trunk, disappearing into the vaulted ceiling.

Caitlin stopped and ran her fingers over the gleaming wood of the curved staircase, tilting her head back to see where it wound its way up to what looked like a loft-style second storey. The house was so far removed from the small suburban townhouse she and Eli rented, it seemed impossible to believe someone could afford to leave such an impressive house sitting empty.

"Don't go upstairs till you've seen the kitchen." Jace disappeared through an archway leaving her and Eli alone in the sitting room.

For a moment there was silence, bar the sounds of cupboards opening and closing in the other room. Caitlin wanted to get excited about the prospect of spending the weekend in such a stunning home, she wanted her husband to get excited with her.

"I didn't know your brother had rich friends," was all she could think to say.

Eli shrugged. "You know Jace." He looked towards the archway where his brother had disappeared. "Everyone loves him." Eli and Jace had an on-again, off-again relationship. Sometimes they seemed close, but in many ways Eli treated Jace like a kid even though he was twenty-eight.

"What do you mean, *everyone loves him*? You sound pissed off."

"Nothing." Eli took hold of her arm just above the elbow. "Come on let's go check out the rest of the house."

Caitlin hesitated. The windows, set high up in the stone walls cast zig-zags of golden light—light that didn't quite reach Eli's face, leaving his expression shadowed and unreadable.

"Come on," his voice flat again. "Don't you want to see how the other half live?"

Caitlin let herself be pulled towards the kitchen, unsure of *what* she'd thought she heard in her husband's voice. They were here now, the three of them together for the weekend, and she was determined to make it a time to remember.

* * *

After exploring the house, the *ooh-ing* and *ah-ing* wound down. As Jace and Eli carried in the rest of their stuff, Caitlin busied herself transferring the contents of the cooler into the fridge. Apart from a few bottles of water, the shelves were empty. Once more, she found herself wondering why someone would need an enormous double fridge in a holiday house. *When you're loaded, why doesn't matter*, she thought with a touch of bitterness. The feeling reminded her of her mother and she immediately pushed it away.

She bent and stacked the beers along the top shelf, then stashed the burgers and buns on the rack underneath. Finally, she dropped the salad into the crisper. With plans to drive into Mandurah for lunch the following day, the only other supplies they'd brought were a few packets of chips and some apples. When the cooler was empty, she stood up and swung the fridge door closed.

"Wanna go for a swim?" Jace stood in the archway, shirtless and wearing a pair of faded-red board shorts hanging low on his hips. His upper body was tanned and muscular from years of working outside.

The shock of seeing him appear out of nowhere made her heart skitter. "Jesus, you scared the crap out of me."

Caitlin took a step backwards and kicked the cooler sending it skidding across the kitchen floor. "Don't creep up on me like that."

"Sorry, Cat. I thought you heard me coming." He held his hands up feigning innocence but couldn't hold onto the concerned expression, a cheeky smile giving him away.

"I don't know why you think jumping out on me is funny." She tried to sound annoyed, but it was difficult to keep a straight face when Jace was laughing. As always, his sunny disposition was infectious. "Stop it." She grabbed a tea towel from the counter and tried to whack him across the arm.

He dodged away before she could land the blow. "You'll have to be quicker than that." He laughed and snatched the cloth from her hand then dangled it over his head.

Caitlin squealed and leaped up trying to grab the towel out of his grasp. They were acting like a pair of children, but it felt good to laugh and have some fun.

"You're gonna get it, if you don't give that back." She grabbed his upraised arm and tried to pull it lower.

"Sounds like the party's already started." Eli stood in the doorway, a bath towel slung over his shoulder. His mouth drawn back in an amused smile that Caitlin could tell was for his brother's benefit.

She let go of Jace's arm and turned back to the fridge looking for something to occupy her hands. Her eyes landed on the esky, it had slid across the room and hit a narrow door on the far right wall. Making a show of retrieving it and securing the lid, she kept her back turned as the brothers discussed taking a swim and having a barbeque. She didn't know why, but the thought of meeting her husband's gaze unsettled her. Maybe because he might see disappointment in her eyes.

A moment ago, she'd been laughing and horsing around with his brother. She'd managed to let go of the sadness and allow herself to feel happy again, until Eli showed up. She realised his presence alone was enough to suck the joy out of her body and leave her feeling ashamed of herself. Even as the thought crossed her mind, she found herself inwardly shrinking with guilt. Eli was grieving. The loss of their baby hit him hard, *did that make him a bad person?*

"Cat, what do you think?" Jace asked, opening the fridge.

"Sounds great." She had no idea what she was agreeing to, but it seemed easier to just go along with whatever the two had planned. She picked up the esky and, with her eyes still on the narrow white door, took a breath. "Where does this door go?" She hadn't meant to ask, the words just slipped out.

"Looks like a pantry." Eli stepped around the long island bench that cut a line of wood and marble through the centre of the kitchen. He stood beside her, she could feel his arm brushing against her shoulder as he reached for the round silver doorknob. He pulled the door open and with it came a gust of cool air. "Huh, I think it's a cellar."

Caitlin leaned forward and caught a whiff of something sour mingled with dust. Beyond the door was darkness. She'd never been in a house with a cellar before. It put her in mind of an old horror movie where an evil book hidden under the house had the power to unleash hell. She shivered and tried to block the image from her mind. If they were going to spend the weekend here, she didn't want to psych herself up into being too terrified to use the kitchen at night. It would only give Eli a reason to remind her he didn't want to come in the first place.

"I told you, the guy's rich. It's probably a wine cellar." Jace snapped the tab on a can of beer and took a swig.

Eli shrugged and pulled the door closed. Just for a second, Caitlin caught a glimpse of a staircase, grey and shadowed. The door clicked shut, cutting off the view.

"It looks like—"

"Go put your bathers on." Eli slid his hand around her waist and guided her away from the door. She wanted to suggest exploring the cellar, thinking it might be more interesting than going for a swim. But there was no mistaking the instructional tone in her husband's voice, or the pressure of his hand on her waist.

She glanced over at Jace but he seemed to be reading the tiny writing on the side of his beer can. "Okay. Won't be long." Her tone sounded meek, even to her own ears.

Upstairs in the room Eli chose for them, Catlin replayed the moment her husband ordered her to go and get changed. She'd been doing it a lot lately; dissecting their every interaction as if searching for a way to figure out what she had to do to make him happy. He'd treated her like a confused child and she went along with it. She felt her cheeks flush with embarrassment. When had that started? She sat on the bed and pulled some clothes out of the travel bag. Eli had already taken his things out of the bag and placed them on top of a dark wood chest of drawers that stood next to the window.

His t-shirts were folded and stacked next to a pair of jeans, with underwear and socks piled on either side. She didn't have to check the ensuite bathroom to know his shaving gear and toiletries would be neatly laid out near the sink. She had no idea why his neatness suddenly annoyed her. *No*, she corrected herself. *It's not suddenly, it's always bothered me.* Only now he barely spoke to her and when he did it was to give an order, was it any wonder his little habits were wearing on her nerves?

She sucked in a deep breath and let it out with a tired sigh. *Things will improve. It just takes time.* Maybe this weekend would loosen them up and she'd see a glimmer of the old Eli. The man who used to call her at work to tell her he missed her, kiss the back of her neck while she cooked dinner. It seemed like another life, a sweeter dreamy time that vanished like a misty morning.

Catlin poked through the clothes she'd scattered on the bed and pulled out her bikini. She'd lost weight. If she were still carrying the baby, she'd be almost full-term by now. She pushed off the bed and stood, refusing to let that train of thought take her into a dark tunnel of despair. Stripping off her clothes, she focused on the evening to come. A barbeque, drinks, maybe even a few laughs.

The bikini fit; a little loose in the seat but not too bad. She ran her fingers through her hair and pulled on her t-shirt and shorts, then slipped her feet into flip-flops. She remembered seeing Eli with a towel over his shoulder and wondered if there was a linen cupboard on the second floor.

The five bedrooms were set out in an L-shape above the sitting room. The linen cupboard turned out to be on the west side of the house almost directly above the entrance. Catlin looked over the array of sheets, blankets, and bath towels. It felt weird to be looking through a stranger's cupboards, almost like spying. Jace said they were free to use whatever they wanted, as long as they washed it and returned it to wherever they found it.

She smacked her lips together and grabbed a powder-blue towel off the middle shelf. As it left the pile, the two towels below it tumbled down.

"Damn." She dropped the blue towel on the floor and bent to pick the others up, but in doing so, kicked one of the towels under the bottom shelf.

"What's taking so long?" There was no mistaking the impatience in Eli's voice. It echoed up from the lower floor with an urgency that bordered on anger.

Catlin left the towels and jogged to the top of the stairs. Below, Eli stood in the centre of the main sitting room, hands on hips and head tilted up. Even at a distance, she could see his brows drawn together like dark angry lines.

"I'll be right down." She leaned over the banister, breathless from rushing. "Just give me a minute." Without waiting for an answer, she turned and jogged back to the linen cupboard.

Once she was out of sight, Caitlin slowed to a walk. A small defiance, but it felt good to make him wait. They had all weekend, it didn't make sense for him to be yelling up the stairs for her to hurry. A lot of things made no sense lately.

She reached the cupboard and scooped up one of the fallen towels, folded it and put it back on the shelf. She had to kneel to reach the second towel. The floor under the bottom shelf felt gritty with dust. She slapped her hand around feeling for the towel when it occurred to her there might be spiders lurking down there. She pulled her hand back and lowered her self until her face was pressed against the bare hard wood floor.

A musty smell wafted up her nostrils. The space under the shelf looked to be a metre or so wide and maybe three-quarters of a metre deep. The towel lay scrunched up near the wall along with a sizable nest of dust bunnies.

"That'll need washing," she spoke aloud even though there was no one to hear her but the dust bunnies. "Cobwebs but no spiders, thank…" She let her words trail off as something on the left side of the cupboard caught her attention.

The panelling between the lower shelf and the floor had a hole in it. Small, no bigger than a finger, it looked smooth and deliberately cut. She turned her head to the right, letting her cheek touch the floor. The other side of the cupboard looked identical, minus the hole. *It could be a pest control thing.* She remembered Eli telling her about trap doors and holes cut into floors for pest control purposes.

She turned back to the hole and slid her hand across the gritty floor, her finger just touching the small dark circle. There could be rat traps and cockroach baits behind the panel. She sucked in her bottom lip trying to decide if opening the trap was a good idea. After all, what did she hope to discover? But that was just it, like the door to the wine cellar, the unknown attracted her. Her pulse raced with excitement.

It might be the guy's porn stash. It seemed a bit extreme to go to such lengths to hide a few DVDs or magazines. On the other hand, maybe he was into some dark kinky stuff and didn't want anyone to find it. She hesitated. If what she found turned out to be really freaky, she didn't know if she wanted to see it.

"Jesus, stop dithering and look," the sound of her voice on the empty landing calmed her, made her fears seem farfetched. Her husband and brother-in-law were just downstairs, whatever she found couldn't hurt her.

Caitlin hooked her finger into the hole and pulled. The panel tilted forwards and came away from the wall with a scrape of wood on wood. A dusty looking cobweb hung across the opening. She grimaced and swatted it away. Even in the almost total blackness, something long and metallic stood out. She put her hand into the cavity and touched the object. It felt cold and smooth. Reaching in a little further, she curled her fingers over the far edge of what she was now certain was a box.

"Caitlin." Eli's voice made her jump. She let go of the box and pulled her hand out of the cavity, rapping her knuckles on the edge of the hole.

"What's going on up there?" His voice came from somewhere below, most likely the foot of the stairs.

Without thinking, she pushed the wooden flap back in place and scrambled up, dragging the dusty towel from under the shelf.

"Coming." She stuffed the dirty towel under a pile of sheets on the middle shelf. Whispering a curse under her breath, she snatched up the blue towel and slung it over her shoulder then closed the cupboard door.

"What were you doing up there?" Eli stood at the foot of the stairs, one hand gripping the banister.

"Toilet emergency."

She stepped down into the sitting room and put her hand on his arm. His skin felt warm, almost hot before he drew away. "You've got something on your face." He jerked his chin towards her.

Caitlin put her hand to her cheek.

"No. The other side."

She brushed at her face and then looked at her hand. There was a fine smear of dirt on her fingers. "Huh. I kicked one of my flip-flops under the bed. Someone really should vacuum under there." She rubbed her fingers together and gave her husband what she hoped was a carefree smile. "Ready for a swim?"

"I've been ready for the last twenty minutes." He turned and stalked through to the kitchen.

* * *

She'd been expecting a swimming pool. Instead, Jace led them through the back door and onto a huge, grey, wooden deck complete with a dome-shaped silver barbeque, padded cane furniture and large spa bath.

"Down there." Jace pointed towards the deep rolling hill where long greenish-yellow grass rippled in the late afternoon sun.

Caitlin put her hand up to shade her eyes. At the foot of the hill, a channel of copper-coloured water glistened. "Is it a lake?" She wasn't sure how she felt about swimming in stagnant water.

"No, it's a runnel that leads to the river." He turned and pointed to where the water disappeared into thick forest. "You can't see it from here, but the Murray River runs in that direction." He turned and smiled down at her. "Don't worry, it's safe as long as the river's not moving too fast."

His skin was golden brown and his blue eyes—so different from Eli's—were wide with excitement. She wondered, not for the first time, how the brothers could be so dissimilar. She caught herself wishing Eli could be more like his untroubled, easy-going sibling. As if Jace could read her thoughts, he smiled. Caitlin looked away hoping he didn't notice the guilty look on her face.

They headed down the hill, Jace in the lead with Eli close on his heels. Caitlin could feel the sweat popping out on the back of her neck and looked forward to plunging into the cold river. At the water's edge, a faded wooden jetty, no more than two metres long, jutted out over the water. On the bank to the left lay an upturned canoe. The three of them crowded together on the end of the jetty peering into the slowly flowing water.

"It looks okay."

Before Caitlin could answer, Jace dropped his towel and leapt off the jetty, landing in the water with a thundering cannonball.

She squealed as cold water sprayed her face and clothes. Without waiting for Eli, she pulled her t-shirt over her head and dropped her shorts. She then sank onto her butt, her legs dangling over the edge of the platform, and lowered herself into the cool copper water. It was just as she'd hoped, fresh without an icy bite, but still enough of a shock to make her body tingle.

Keeping her chin above the water, she swam towards the middle of the narrow channel. Ahead of her, Jace floated on his back staring at the sky. She stole a quick glance back at the jetty and saw Eli standing watching her. Part of her wanted to call to him, but it seemed like that was all she ever did anymore; beg for his involvement. Instead, she turned away and concentrated on the moment, letting the soothing water lap at her neck, enjoying the feeling of weightlessness.

"If I give you a three stroke head start, do you reckon you could beat me back to the jetty?" Jace called to her from a few metres away, his blond hair sticking out from his head in wet spikes.

"Make it four strokes and you've got a race." She knew Eli would be watching and listening from the shore, but didn't care. She felt excited and happy splashing around in the water. If only for a short while, she wanted to forget she was a thirty-one-year-old married woman with a sullen, disinterested husband and a failed attempt at becoming a mother.

As Jace approached, she turned and faced the jetty. Eli had moved to the small patch of sandy bank and was wading into the water, but hadn't taken the plunge. Seeing him there made her pause.

"Do you want to join the race?" She paddled her feet and raised her upper body out of the water, one hand in the air.

"Yeah." Jace joined in from behind her. "Get involved." Eli shook his head and Caitlin felt her heart sink, just a little. "Don't be scared, mate," Jace teased. "I'll give you the same head start as your wife."

To her surprise, Eli laughed and waded into the water. Soon the three of them were lined up in the centre of the channel.

"Right." Jace, in the middle, looked first at Caitlin and then at Eli. "On the count of three, Cat gets four strokes. Okay?"

They both nodded. When Jace reached three, Caitlin lunged forward, arms thumping only to feel both her ankles being grabbed. Before she knew what was happening, Jace and Eli pulled her backwards and both men took off.

"You sneaky bastards," Catlin spluttered in mock outrage and took off after them.

By the time she reached the jetty the three of them were laughing. "I can't believe you fell for it." Jace wrapped one arm around the small metal ladder that hung from the platform while Eli, still grinning and panting, held onto the end of the jetty. Water ran down his face in tiny rivets, his teeth looked startlingly white against his tanned skin.

Caitlin swam up next to him and placed her arm over his shoulder letting the gentle movement of the river push her body against his.

"You two are devious." She laughed and stroked the back of his neck, enjoying the feel of his wet skin against hers.

His free hand slid down her back and then gripped her waist. For a second it seemed as if he were going to kiss her. A shiver of excitement worked its way from her stomach to her chest. Almost as much as the closeness they'd shared, Caitlin missed the physical contact. But instead of embracing her, his hand pushed her away. It was a soft push, but the rejection hit her hard.

Eli turned and pulled himself up onto the jetty. "I'm going to see if I can get the barbie started." He walked down the platform, dripping shorts slapping his thighs. He moved without a backward glance, only stopping to pick up his flip-flops and towel.

Tears mingled with water from her wet hair, running down her cheeks. A tightness filled her chest, burning, as a sob caught somewhere between her stomach and throat.

That small movement, his hand pushing her away, encapsulated all the minor slights and rebuffs of the past months. She looked away from the hill where Eli moved towards the house and found herself staring into Jace's clear blue eyes.

She could see by the surprised look on his face he'd witnessed what had happened. The pain of rejection, now mingled with embarrassment, made her want to plunge under the water and never come up for air. All she could do was look away and swipe at the tears with her wet hand.

"You deserve better," his voice, husky and low, at odds with his usual playful chatter.

For a moment, she found herself at a loss for words. The water, at first refreshing, now made her shiver. "Thanks." She reached for the ladder not knowing what else to say.

Climbing the few steps to the jetty seemed exhausting. When she reached the top, Caitlin scooped up her towel and wrapped it around herself. As she reached for her clothes, Jace climbed out of the water and stood beside her. For a moment neither of them spoke. She felt exposed and embarrassed.

"He's always been moody." Jace touched her arm. In spite of being in the water, his fingers were warm. "It's nothing you've done."

Caitlin had the urge to throw herself into his arms, to feel them wrap around her and chase the cold away. Instead, she wrapped her arms around herself and nodded. Jace had always been kind, much kinder than his brother, and right now, she needed kindness.

"I think he blames me, you know, about the baby." It was the first time she'd mention her miscarriage in months and yet here she was talking to Jace of all people about something she'd never even shared with her friends.

"Don't think that. It's… It's Eli's problem, not yours. He's blind to what he has, that's his mistake." His hand, still on her arm, moved slowly down to her hand. "Come on." He took her hand and began leading her towards the house. "You should put some clothes on and warm up."

Caitlin allowed herself to be pulled up the hill towards the house. They walked through the long grass without speaking. When they neared the deck where Eli stood fiddling with the barbeque, they let go of each other's hands.

Chapter Two

The sun sank in a blaze of orange and purple, smearing the sky with fading colour. Apart from the lights on the deck, the rear of the property washed into night. Caitlin, reclining in a thickly padded grey and black cane-chair, sipped from a can of beer. The sour liquid hit the back of her throat almost making her gag. She wished they'd brought a bottle of wine with them, at least then she'd have something worth drinking.

She leaned forward and dumped the can next to the plate containing her half-eaten burger. Thinking about wine put her in mind of the cellar. If Jace was right and it was for wine, it might be worth exploring. She decided to wait until the brothers were asleep and sneak down for a look.

"Didn't you like the burger?" Eli had spent the last half an hour talking Jace's ear off about politics, but now it seemed he was interested in what she ate.

"Not hungry." She didn't even try to make conversation. That moment in the water still burned like an insect bite that couldn't be soothed. She waited for him to say more but he simply shrugged and turned back to his brother. But Jace was too quick for him.

"I've got something that'll help with your appetite."
He stood and reached into the top pocket of his shirt. He
held up a skinny-looking joint and then slipped it between
his lips.

"What the fuck, Jace." Eli frowned, scrunching up his
lips as if he'd tasted something nasty. "You're too old to
be mucking around with that shit."

Ignoring him, Jace patted the pockets on his baggy tan
shorts until he found his lighter. "What do you say, Cat?"

"Love to." She stood and crossed the deck, then to
Jace's surprise, she plucked the joint out of his mouth and
put it between her lips. "Light it up."

A broad grin spread across her brother-in-law's face
as he flicked on the lighter and lit the joint. Caitlin took a
long pull, filling her lungs with smoke then coughing it out
again.

Eli tutted loudly and let his head tip back as if the
sight of his wife and brother smoking a spliff was more
than his eyes could stand. Caitlin laughed and handed the
joint to Jace. She could see her husband disapproved, in
fact, the disgusted look on his face gave her a flicker of
satisfaction. She'd spent months tip-toeing around him,
trying to win his affection back in any way possible. Never
really understanding what she'd done to repel him in the
first place. And after every rebuff, she kept crawling back
desperate for his approval. Well, not anymore.

Jace handed her the joint, his face partially obscured
by a cloud of smoke. She took it and walked to the edge of
the deck, sinking down with her legs dangling over the
side. There was a slight breeze, she could hear it rustling
the trees. Insects chirped, unseen in the blackness.

"Come on, mate, loosen-up." She heard Jace talking
to his brother. Again she found herself comparing Eli to
Jace, wishing he could be more like his younger brother.

"Don't coax him." She felt tired, limbs heavy with a
weariness born of trying to keep up the pretence of
normality. "He doesn't want to be here. Can't you see

that?" She spoke over her shoulder, refusing to turn around and meet Eli's condemning gaze.

"I'm going to bed." A creak from the sofa told her Eli was on his feet. "Don't let her do anything stupid." The lack of feeling in his voice was worse than the disapproval.

She heard the back door clang shut and then only the chirping of insects and the distant chatter of wild ducks as they settled for the night. This time there were no tears. She wouldn't spend another night crying over a man who clearly felt nothing but distaste for her.

Her attempts at patching up their dying relationship seemed pathetic, almost juvenile. Had she really believed a weekend away would magically drive her indifferent husband back into her arms? She looked down at her legs, pale but still shapely. Even after his obvious rejection at the river, she'd put on the rust-coloured sundress for the barbeque because Eli once told her the colour suited her, making her look otherworldly. She put the joint to her lips and sucked in another drag, letting the harsh smoke hit the back of her throat.

Jace's feet moved over the deck, his flip-flops smacking against his soles as though he were running, a silly thought, she realised. When he flopped down next to her on the edge of the deck, she almost asked him why he'd been running, but stopped herself knowing it was a crazy thing to say.

"You okay?" He slid his fingers over her hand, his movements laconic and heavy. She opened her mouth to ask him what he was doing when his fingers closed over the joint and plucked it from her grasp.

"I'm…" she hesitated, wondering how to answer. "I'm waking up." The words came out slowly, but made perfect sense. She laughed, not sure what was so funny— suddenly the whole situations struck her as comical.

Jace joined her and the two of them were howling and nudging each other.

"You've had enough of this," he said, grinding the joint out on the edge of the deck. For some reason, his voice sounded hollow as if he were speaking through a tube.

Caitlin covered her mouth with her hand and tried to suppress a hiccupping laugh. "You know what we should do?" She turned to her brother-in-law and grabbed his arm. His blue eyes looked hooded and sleepy. "We should go down to the wine cellar and get a bottle." She gave his arm a slight shake to emphasise the brilliance of the idea.

He didn't answer straight away, just blinked and stared at her. She thought he hadn't heard her, so she tried again. "We should go down–"

"Good idea." Jace stood and offered her his hand. Her thoughts were a little hazy, but it struck her that they had spent a lot of time holding hands today. She almost didn't put her hand in his, wavering for a second. The image of Eli walking away from her on the jetty popped into her mind. She could almost hear the furious flapping of his wet shorts and feel the way her cheeks burned with humiliation. Without further hesitation, she pressed her palm against Jace's and let him pull her to her feet.

By the time they entered the house and reached the cellar door, her thoughts began to level out a little. She pulled her hand free and rubbed it on her dress. If Jace noticed, he gave no indication. He took hold of the silver knob and pushed the door open. Her mind snapped back to the hidden compartment under the bottom shelf of the linen cupboard and the sleek looking metal box sitting amongst cobwebs and dust bunnies. If there were things hidden in the cellar, did she really want to know?

Jace stepped through the door and ran his hand over the wall to his left. "There's a light switch."

The small space at the top of the stairs morphed into weak yellow light. Caitlin didn't move from her spot near the door. Exploring the cellar seemed like a good idea five minutes ago, but now she wasn't sure she wanted to venture under the house. She turned and looked back at the kitchen. Something about the layout of the building had bothered her since they first arrived and now it dawned on her. The windows, or lack of. The only windows in the place were set up high in the walls. Even the kitchen lacked natural light.

"Huh."

She watched Jace's expression as he looked downwards. He seemed to be surprised by what he saw.

"What's wrong?" She could feel sweat build on her upper lip and swiped at it with the back of her hand. "Is there something down there?" She didn't know why she was whispering. Eli was upstairs, probably asleep by now. Apart from the two of them, there was no one to disturb, but still she felt reluctant to raise her voice.

He turned back to her. Under the yellow light his face looked washed out and stark. "Nothing wrong, just not what I was expecting." Before she had the chance to question him further, he'd already disappeared down the stairs. Caitlin followed him into the cellar.

When she reached the top of the stairs, she understood what Jace meant by *not what I was expecting*. The room below looked bare and unremarkable. A couple of free-standing wine racks were pushed against the wall on the right, their shelves almost bare save for a handful of bottles. She tasted the stale, hot air and moved down a few steps noticing coarse concrete flooring and a stack of cardboard cartons piled near the wine racks, but otherwise the room was empty.

She should have been relieved, but felt only disappointment. *Am I that desperate for excitement?* Like a child, she'd hoped to find a monster under the stairs. It would be funny if it wasn't so tragic.

She didn't bother going lower, instead she sat down on the step and watched Jace pull bottles out of the rack. "I don't know anything about wine, is this stuff expensive?"

She tucked the hem of her dress under her legs and leaned her elbows on her knees. "Give me a look." She'd lost interest in the wine, not really caring if they found a bottle they could drink or not. What she really wanted now was to go to sleep and, with any luck, block out her problems for a few hours.

Jace moved towards the stairs. He held the bottle up towards her with the label turned so she could read it.

"Nothing special." She scanned the bottle noting the familiar logo. "We can easily replace it when we go into Mandurah."

"That's weird."

"Not really," she spoke without looking up. "Just because he's rich doesn't mean he has to be into fancy wine."

"No." The edge to Jace's usually calm voice caught her attention. "There's a door." He pointed to the area behind the stairs.

Caitlin put the bottle on the stair below her feet and stood. She turned and half bent to look around the staircase. Set into the far corner of the wall was a door. She could only see glimpses of it between the slats of the staircase, but there was no mistaking the bolt and padlock just above the handle. Her stomach flipped as though she were inside a fast-moving elevator.

Jace left her standing on the step nearest the floor and went towards the newly discovered door.

"Don't open it," she whispered, stepping down.

"I *can't* open it, it's locked." His voice sounded tight, almost anxious. She didn't think she'd ever heard him sound so grown-up.

He stopped, blocking the door with his body. For a moment, neither of them spoke. He bent over, examining the lock. Caitlin clutched the hem of her dress, wanting him to come away from the door so they could go upstairs and pretend they'd never found the locked room.

"I don't like this, Jace. Let's just leave it and go upstairs." Beneath the stale air, she could smell something else, a sour odour that reminded her of sweat. "Jace," she raised her voice just above a whisper.

To her relief, he turned and walked back to the stairs. "There's no way we're getting in there without a crowbar." He shrugged his shoulders. "It's probably where he keeps valuables and stuff he doesn't want to leave lying around the house."

Caitlin let out a breath. As much as she wanted a distraction, the cellar unsettled her. Maybe whatever the owner kept behind the locked door was better left alone.

"We probably shouldn't even be down here." Maybe it was the joint affecting her, but she felt edgy, eager to be out of the hot, stale air that filled the small space.

"No arguments from me." Jace's eyes looked glassy under the yellow lights, he seemed jittery as if being under the house in a confined space bothered him as much as her.

Caitlin turned and clamoured up the steps, forgetting the bottle of wine she'd set down until her bare foot kicked it and sent it crashing over the side of the stairs. The bottle hit the concrete, exploding on impact in shower of fractured shards and splattered liquid. The sound was so loud in the silent cellar that Caitlin could hear the clang of glass reverberating in her ears.

"Holy shit." Jace stared up at her, his mouth open in surprise.

For a second, she was too stunned to speak. The mess from the bottle covered at least a quarter of the floor space with the acrid smell of wine now filling the room.

Jace must have read the look on her face. His surprise turned into concern. "It's okay, Cat. I think I saw a sweeping brush on the deck, I'll–"

A clearly audible scraping sound followed by a thump, cut through Jace's words. Both he and Caitlin turned towards the locked door. Silence followed, only broken by

Jace's rapid breathing. They waited. Caitlin felt her nails digging into her palms and realised she'd curled her hands into tight fists.

"Maybe it was—"

The scrape came again, louder this time, as if long nails were being dragged across a gritty floor. Jace turned to her, his mouth set in a tight line. He looked younger than his twenty-eight years, uncertain as if waiting for her to speak.

"It might be an animal." She took a step down, drawing closer to her brother-in-law. "You know," she whispered now almost level with his ear. "Trapped in there or something…" She let her words trail off waiting for him to agree.

He turned back to the door. "Stay here," his voice wavered but he stepped away from the staircase and moved towards the door.

Caitlin wanted to grab his sleeve and pull him back but he was out of reach, moving across the confined space of the cellar, taking cautious steps as if ready to jump back if something moved. When he reached the door, he side-stepped, reminding her of the way TV cops get ready to burst through doors. For an insane second, she almost laughed, but the sound dried up in her throat.

Jace looked back at her, she gritted her teeth and nodded. *We'll be laughing about this in the morning. It'll turn out to be a rat and we'll laugh.* Even as the thought ran through her mind, she didn't quite believe it.

He raised his hand and rapped on the door. Two sharp knocks bounced off the wood sounding incredibly loud in the silent room. Almost instantly, something bumped against the other side of the door. Jace flinched and drew his hand back as Caitlin gasped and shoved her clenched fist against her lips.

"Is someone there?" came Jace's deep, steady voice.

A moment passed in silence. She held her breath listening for any sound and then when it seemed too much time had passed, she let out a breath. In the same instant a muffled response came from behind the locked door. Not so much a reply but more like a muted groan.

"There's someone in there." Jace turned to her, blinking rapidly. "I think someone's locked in there."

"Oh God, what should we do?" Despite the hot stale air, she felt cold, as if an icy finger touched her spine.

"Go get Eli."

Chapter Three

"Wake-up." Caitlin's throat felt dry, as if the words were trapped behind a layer of air.

She flicked the lights on, not bothering to wait for her husband to respond. She crossed the room, leaping on the bed. Bouncing the mattress under her weight, she grabbed his shoulder.

"Turn the lights off," his voice was slurred with sleep, his head buried deep in the pillows.

"Get-up, Eli, something's happened." She jerked his arm trying to pull him towards her. Any other time, she'd hesitate to wake him, knowing how grumpy he'd be if raised from a deep sleep. But her husband's mood was the last thing on her mind. For once she didn't give a damn how angry Eli would be.

"What's wrong?" He sounded impatient, as if speaking to a panicky child. She had the sudden urge to slap him on his bare shoulder but pulled her hand away and stood up.

"Will you stop asking questions and get the fuck out of bed." He sat up and faced her, eyes blinking at the light. He looked like he was about to protest, but something, most likely the panic on her face stopped him. He threw back the sheet and got up.

"Okay. I'm coming."

Satisfied he was following, Caitlin turned and raced back to the stairs. Jace was alone in the cellar, if whoever was behind the door got out, he could be in real danger. She knew the door was secured with a padlock, but to her mind it made no difference. Something was terribly wrong and whichever way she looked at it, things were about to get worse.

"What's going on?"

Eli's feet pounded down the stairs behind her, but she kept going. "Caitlin, will you stop and tell me what's happened?"

He caught up with her at the archway leading to the kitchen and grabbed her arm. "Has something happened to Jace?" He was out of breath, panting. Wearing only shorts, his chest looked pale in the light that spilled from the kitchen into the darkened sitting room. Even in the shadows, she could see the fear in his eyes. In an instant, all the bitterness she felt towards him that day evaporated and she wanted to put her arms around him.

"No." She put her hand over his. "He's fine. At least he was when I left him." She kept moving towards the cellar door, pulling him along with her. "There's someone in the cellar." She could see the confusion on his face but didn't know how else to explain. "Just come down there with me and see for yourself." She stopped at the open door and pointed at the stairs.

Eli hesitated. His dark hair stood up in clumps, a creased line ran down his cheek from where it had been pressed into the pillow. She wasn't used to seeing him look unsure of himself, it rattled her. He was supposed to be the mature one, the guy with all the answers.

"He's down there on his own." She tried to steady her voice, but couldn't hide her anxiety.

He blinked once as if waking up to the moment for the first time, then nodded and headed down the stairs.

At the foot of the stairs, Eli paused. She could see him staring at the smashed remnants of the wine, his eyes narrowed and he glanced over his shoulder not quite meeting her gaze. She felt a quiver of guilt blossoming in her chest. It was obvious what she and Jace had been doing in the cellar and she had no doubt that in her husband's mind she was already to blame for whatever was about to be played out.

Jace appeared at the bottom of the stairs, his face bleached under the artificial yellow light.

"There's someone locked in there." He pointed towards the door. "We heard them moving and trying to speak." He glanced up at Caitlin looking for confirmation.

"He's right, there's someone on the other side of that door," her own voice, high and breathless. She wanted Eli to say or do something, to take charge and tell them what to do next. It fleetingly occurred to her that she should suggest finding something to prise the door open with, but the words stuck in her throat.

"It's probably a possum or something." Eli, not wearing shoes, moved past his brother and side-stepped the broken glass. He approached the door without hesitation. "The thing probably came in through the roof and ended up trapped."

"It's not a possum." Jace followed him to the door and stood next to his brother.

Caitlin wanted to believe Eli's reasoning but couldn't see how an animal could make its way from the roof to a room under the house. Even if it managed to get inside the wall cavity, there was no way it could end up down in the cellar.

"If we break the door open and it turns out to be rats or something, how's your mate going to react?" Eli took hold of the padlock and gave it a yank as if to make his point.

"This is stupid." Jace threw up his hands. "It's not an animal." He stepped around his brother and banged on the door using the side of his fist. The thumping of his hand was so loud, Caitlin flinched.

They waited. The three of them silent, straining to hear movement from the other side of the door. After thirty seconds of nothing, Eli shrugged. "I can't believe you got me out of bed for–"

His words were cut off by a groan that started strong and then turned into a muffled thump.

Jace was the first to react. "I'm finding something to smash that lock." He pushed past his brother and began pulling open the cardboard cartons stacked haphazardly next to the wine rack.

Eli hesitated for a second before joining the search. Caitlin's heart beat in her throat. She had no idea what would happen when they smashed the lock, but a feeling of pressure built in the enclosed space. It reminded her of the day she lost the baby. The situation was completely different but the sickening dread blossoming in her chest, growing tighter by the minute, felt all too familiar.

She realised she was clenching her fists again and forced her hands to relax. She couldn't just stand by and watch, not if there really was someone who needed help. There was nothing she could have done when her baby slipped away, maybe this time she could make a difference. But how?

Closing her eyes, she tried to focus on what they needed. Something sturdy and solid, long enough to wedge under the bolt, not the padlock. It would be easier to wrench the sliding bolt off than attempt to smash the padlock. Retracing her steps since entering the house, she scoured her memory, moving slowly from the point where they first explored the house.

They'd checked out the kitchen first then the study just off the main sitting room. She recalled admiring the desk, an oversized dark wood antique with a maroon blotter. An old-fashioned chaise lounge sat opposite the door upholstered in the same shade of leather as the blotter. As her mind sifted through each room, including the bedrooms, something nagged at her memory.

An image popped into her mind with the speed of a bullet. The fireplace. She turned and raced up the stairs, running through the kitchen so fast she almost lost her footing as she rounded the island bench.

The lights in the main room were off; only a short arc of illumination spilled through from the kitchen. With no idea where the switch was located, her only option was to move slowly and dodge the shadowy hulks of furniture.

Edging her way forward, Caitlin bent slightly with her arms out feeling her way past what she knew from memory was a large brown leather couch. She moved around the first obstacle and towards the centre of the room. With no moonlight or street lamps, nothing but blackness spilled through the high windows. All she could see were outlines, the largest, in the centre of the room, had to be the fireplace. She shuffled forward expecting to feel the lip of the grate with her bare toes.

Another metre or so and her shin collided with something solid. The impact was minor, little more than a bump, but it smarted. She winced and rubbed her leg, if she'd been going any faster, it could have been a lot more painful.

"Where are you?" she asked into the darkness.

A few more steps and her toe made contact with something raised. Dropping to her knees, she slapped her hands around the floor and felt the five-centimetre lip that fronted the fireplace. She gave a little laugh, more of relief than triumph, and began feeling around. Flapping her hand to the left, she encountered nothing but the curved edge of the dome. Changing direction, her wrist hit something that gave a metal on metal *ching*.

"Yes." She hadn't noticed the fire tool set when they first arrived, but her gut told her that where there's an open fire, there's bound to be tools.

She took hold of the set, the iron implements hanging from a free-standing frame, clanged together making a ringing sound like an old-time dinner gong. She ran her fingers up and down the various tools until she found the one with the pointed end. She lifted the poker off the frame with a tiny flicker of satisfaction. Maybe she wasn't completely helpless after all.

It was easier making her way back to the kitchen, all she had to do was head for the light and avoid the sofa and coffee table. By the time she entered the cellar, she could hear Eli's voice harsh with frustration.

"That'll never work. We need something longer that won't bend."

She clamoured down the stairs and picked her way around the broken glass.

"Try this." She held the poker out, its point dangling towards the floor.

Seemingly unaware of her presence, Eli continued to work at the lock using what looked like a letter opener. Jace turned to face her his eyes brightening when he saw the poker.

"Perfect. Where did you find it?"

"I remembered the fireplace and thought there had to be a poker." She handed him the fire tool. "I thought it might be easier to ram the point under the bolt and try to prise it off."

"Yeah, good idea." He gave her an appreciative nod and then turned the poker so he could examine the point.

"What's a good idea?" Eli turned away from the door, his face shiny with sweat. "Oh yeah, perfect." He nodded to the tool in his brother's hand. "That should do the trick. Here, let me." He held out his hand.

"No. I'll do it." He didn't often refuse his brother. Caitlin could see the surprise on Eli's face. She wondered what went on while she was upstairs, but knew now wasn't the time to ask.

Jace wedged the poker under the thick steel bolt and rocked it towards himself like a lever. He pulled with enough force to make his already impressive biceps bulge under the effort. She heard him grunt and a second later came the ragged creak of wood splintering. She stepped closer and stood beside her husband. There had been a time when she'd have reached for his hand, but it seemed those days were over.

She felt her nails digging into her palms again but didn't care. Sweat hung from the blond hair on the back of Jace's neck. With one final grunt, he forced the entire bolt away from the wood. It swung down, held only by the two remaining screws that secured one side of the thing to the door frame.

Jace swiped at his forehead with his left forearm. She could see the smear of perspiration on his skin. Still holding the poker in his right hand, he turned to look at her and Eli.

"Ready?"

Eli nodded. "Be careful."

Catlin didn't know what she thought would happen when he opened the door. A small part of her still wanted to believe a possum would come scampering out. But she kept remembering the scraping sound. That slow drag of something heavy and deliberate hadn't come from a small animal.

Jace turned back to the door and grasped the knob. He moved his wrist as if to turn it but then let it go so he could wipe his hand on the front of his shirt. When he finally turned the knob, the door swung inwards with surprising ease. Caitlin gasped and clutched Eli's shoulder.

An arm, as grey as the concrete floor beneath it, lay in the arc of light flooding in from the cellar. The first thing that struck Caitlin was how dirty the hand and nails looked. The skin appeared bruised and powdery as if it had been dragged through the dirt.

"Holy shit." Jace took a step into the room running his hand along the wall.

"Watch it, mate. They might try something." Eli's voice sounded croaky and strange, as if coming from someone older.

The lights came on giving them their first real look at the previously locked room.

* * *

"Is he alive?" Her words hung in the air as the three of them regarded the figure on the floor.

"He's breathing." Jace hesitated over the slumped form, not sure whether to touch him.

Caitlin understood his reluctance. From what she could see, the man was in pretty bad shape. He'd clearly been beaten—badly. With half his face pressed to the floor, what she *could* see was a network of cuts and bruises. His eye, swollen shut beneath a gash that sliced through his eyebrow. He wore what looked like jeans and a t-shirt, although the layer of dirt and possibly blood that coated him made it difficult to be sure.

The rawness of the man's appearance made him seem somehow less human. She felt repulsed by him in a way that took her by surprise. He was obviously in need of help yet she felt herself wanting to turn away.

"Who could have done this?" Jace crouched over the man, still not touching him.

"What do you mean, *who*?" Eli's voice, loud and thick with anger cut through their questions. "It's obvious *who*. Your rich mate." He stepped through the doorway and stood over his brother and the unconscious man. "We're in the guy's house, so this has got to be down to him." He pointed at the figure. "What the hell have you got us into?"

Jace looked from Caitlin to Eli, his face slack with shock and confusion. "What? I don't… You think I know something about this?" He shook his head. "You don't really think I knew this was going on?" He turned from his brother back to Caitlin. "Come on."

She didn't know what to say. Eli was right. The house belonged to Jace's friend. She didn't believe for a minute Jace would be involve in hurting someone, but he had to know what sort of man his friend was. Or at least who the guy on the floor was.

"Cat, you don't think I knew about this, do you?" There was an edge of desperation in his voice, it stabbed at her heart.

"No. No, of course I don't. It's just," she hesitated.

"It doesn't matter what she thinks," Eli cut in. "This is serious. We need to get this guy help. Call an ambulance. He might be dying for all we know."

"Please." The one word hung in the air, raw and laboured.

For a second, no one moved. Jace was the first to react and break the spell.

"It's okay, mate. We're gonna get you out of here." He got down on one knee and put his hand on the man's chest. "What's your name?"

It was difficult to tell where the bruising ended and the grime began. One eye was nothing more than a swollen bulb with a slit that was once an eye socket. He tried to speak; moving his lower lip opened up a split that immediately bubbled with blood.

"It's okay." Jace's voice was gentle. "You don't have to say anything now."

Caitlin kept shifting her gaze between the man and Eli, waiting for him to react and take charge. As if reading her thoughts, he turned to her. "Go get a blanket. We need to get him upstairs."

She nodded. Before turning and rushing back upstairs, she took one final look. Beyond the figure on the floor and her husband and brother-in-law, lay the room where the man had been kept. In the far corner, a steel toilet was bolted to the floor. Plastered across the back wall in slashes and dollops were brownish stains. The scene was stark in the unforgiving light of one bare bulb, as if the whole thing were unreal in some way.

She narrowed her eyes, fascinated by the odd pigments decorating the wall. When it dawned on her what she was seeing, her stomach clenched as if she'd been punched. It wasn't paint or damp, but blood. She raised a hand to her mouth as if expecting a scream.

"Caitlin." Eli's voice snapped her gaze off the wall. "Go find a blanket, as quick as you can." His voice was soft, almost as gentle as his brother's. How long had it been since he'd spoken to her with such kindness?

"Okay. Sorry." She turned and fled.

Once on the second floor, Caitlin raced into her bedroom and pulled on a pair of black tennis shoes. She thought of just grabbing a blanket off the bed where Eli had been sleeping, but something else occurred to her. She headed for the linen cupboard stopping only to flick on the lights.

Kneeling in front of the open cupboard, she pressed her cheek to the floorboards. Whatever was in the silver box might be connected to the man in the cellar. After all, someone had gone to great lengths to hide it. *Just like that guy downstairs.* The splattered wall danced across her mind with its gruesome patterns.

She sucked in air through her nostrils and forced the image away. Hooking her finger through the hole in the panel under the bottom shelf, she pulled. She had the box in her hands. A set of clips secured the lid. She flicked them back and opened the box.

A gasp whistled past her lips. Sitting on a cushioned bed of black foam was a gun. Its barrel, sleek and silver glinted in the light. Below the black hand grip, a dark rectangle. She'd seen enough movies to recognise the shape as a clip, something used to hold bullets. *What the hell is this place?*

A shiver made its way up her spine and sent a tremor through her shoulders. Something was terribly wrong. If the brutalized man in the cellar wasn't enough, the sight of the hand gun confirmed it. *Where would someone even get a hand gun?* This wasn't America. Hand guns were almost impossible to procure.

She stared at the gun, the first real one she'd ever seen. Like the blood splatters, it seemed surreal. She flipped the box closed and stood, grabbing a yellow blanket from one of the shelves. She slid the box under her arm, surprised at how weighty it felt and returned to the stairs.

The lights came on when she was half way down, flooding the sitting room. Jace stood in the archway leading to the kitchen, one arm hooked under the guy's armpit as his right arm hung limply over Jace's shoulder. The man's legs bowed out as if he were sinking into the floor.

Eli appeared from the study. "Bring him in here." He crossed the room and shouldered some of the guy's weight. Together, the brothers shuffled the man into the study.

Caitlin began to follow then stopped. She wondered if it were a good idea to mention the gun in front of the injured man. He was hurt and locked in the cellar, but what else did they know about him? How was he connected to the gun? For all she knew it might be his. It seemed in this house, anything could be possible.

She put the box on the coffee table and then changed her mind. Clutching it to her side, she scanned the sitting room, looking for a place to stash the weapon. Deciding upon the sofa, she bent down and slid the silver case between the front legs. There would be time to tell Eli about its existence later.

She could smell him before she entered the study. An earthy odour mixed with sweat and something metallic, it reminded her of a memory she'd pushed so far to the back of her mind, it was now difficult to grasp and identify. She wrinkled her nose and stepped into the room.

The man lay slumped on the chaise lounge. His one visible eye fluttered open as she entered. "Here." Caitlin held the blanket out to her husband, not wanting to have to touch the man herself.

Eli took the blanket without looking at her and draped it over the man's body, tucking it around his shoulders. Jace stood nearby, hands on hips. "We need to get him to a hospital."

Eli nodded. "If my phone worked, we could call an ambulance." There was sarcasm in his voice, clearly aimed at her. Caitlin would have felt wounded by his tone if she wasn't so preoccupied with the gun and the memories that were trying to surface.

"Water." It was only the second time he'd spoken. His eye, brown and watery shifted but didn't focus.

Caitlin turned to her husband. "Why don't you get it?" she spoke before Eli had the chance to order her back to the kitchen. Not because she wanted to remain with the injured man, but more to pre-empt another trip around the house on her own. Something was terribly wrong here, she could feel it in the marrow of her bones. The last thing she wanted was to make any more grim discoveries.

Eli's head snapped in her direction. He seemed to be about to argue, but then change his mind. "Okay." He nodded to the man on the chaise. "Keep an eye on him."

"Are you okay?" Jace asked. He was looking at Caitlin. She wondered fleetingly why he'd waited for Eli to leave the room before asking her, but the thought sank under a wave of emotion.

"I—Are you?" She didn't know how to answer and could feel tears threatening to well up. *Am I so starved of kindness that it only takes one question to break me?*

"Pretty weird, huh?" He rubbed a hand across his forehead.

"Yeah. It's weird all right." She found herself staring at the injured man's face. There was a crescent-shaped bruise on his cheek as if he'd been kicked. She shuddered and looked away. "What's his name?"

"I don't know." Jace shrugged. "You heard me ask, but he—"

"No. I don't mean him." Caitlin jerked her shoulder towards the guy on the chaise. "I'm talking about the man that owns this house."

"Oh yeah. Micky. Micky Blyte." Jace's eyes shifted from her to the doorway.

He was hiding something, she could see it in the way he moved his weight from one foot to the other. It wasn't the first time she'd noticed the tell-tale movement. Now that she thought about it, he'd done the same thing when they arrived and she asked him what the owner did for a living, only then she'd been too distracted, worried about Eli's sombre mood.

"So, what do you know about this Micky Blyte?" said Eli from behind her.

"He's dangerous." The guy on the chaise spoke through swollen lips, his voice thick and sluggish. "We need to get out of here before he comes back."

Chapter Four

Things were spinning out of control. What started out as a harmless idea, a bit of fun, had turned into something Jace could never have imagined. Now everyone looked to him for answers, especially Eli.

"Wait a minute." He could see the panic growing in Cat's eyes. He had to get the situation under control. "We don't even know your name." He spoke to the man lying on the chaise. "How did you end up locked in the cellar?"

"Can I have some water please?" The man held out a tremulous hand to Eli who gave Jace a warning look before handing the guy the bottle he'd retrieved from the kitchen.

The three of them waited while the injured man put the bottle to his swollen lips, winced and then drank. "My name's Felix Holly." He took another sip before continuing. "I don't know why I was in the cellar, only that the man who put me there is crazy." His one functioning eye shifted from Jace to Eli.

"Does it matter who put him there?" Cat stepped closer to Eli. Jace thought he noticed his brother flinch slightly as if her closeness offended him. Knowing the real reason behind Eli's reaction didn't make it any easier to watch.

"We should just get in the car and go." Cat raised her hand as if to touch Eli's arm, but instead brushed a strand of hair off her cheek. "Something's going on here. Something dangerous. We should just go." She turned to Eli. "We can drive to the police station in Mandurah and let them sort it out."

Panic jolted through Jace. If the police got involved, then everything would come to light and he'd find himself in deep shit. He tried to think of another way out of the jam, but his mind ticked back and forth between images of cop cars and blue flashing sirens.

"Just drop me off at the hospital, I'll get them to call the cops from there." He clamped a hand over his abdomen and grimaced. "You got me out of that room. There's no need to get involved in this any further."

Jace felt a glimmer of hope. Maybe there was a way out that wouldn't end with the three of them sitting in a jail cell. "Okay. We'll get you to a–"

"No." Eli's voice was flat. Jace knew that tone all too well. When his brother made up his mind, he wouldn't be moved.

Jace noticed Cat's shoulders droop. Like him, she knew there would be no point in arguing. He wished, just for once, Eli didn't have to always be the one in charge. Jace loved his brother, or at least he used to. Lately it was getting harder to see past the things he did. The way he treated Cat.

"I'm not getting in a car with you until I have some answers." He crossed his arms over his chest and fixed his eyes on Felix. "What's going on here?"

Felix took another sip from the water bottle. Jace couldn't help noticing that he seemed to be feeling a lot better than when they found him slumped on the cellar floor.

"I didn't know his name." He nodded towards Jace. "Not until you said it a minute ago. All I know is he was waiting for me when I left the public swimming pool." He touched a finger to his swollen eye. "It was dark, he came out of nowhere and hit me with something. I didn't really get a good look at him until he got me back here." His voice, slushy through swollen lips, rasped with the effort of speaking. "I don't know how long I've been down there, a few days, maybe longer. It's all a blur."

"And the bruises?" Eli prompted.

Felix let out a long breath as if gathering the courage to continue. "The first day, he started hitting me. He'd put something over his hand so the blows hurt but didn't break the skin. I was groggy from the whack on my head, but I could tell this wasn't the first time he'd done something like this." He shook his head. Jace noticed there were grazes on the man's neck. "He's crazy, he gets off on inflicting pain. He kept waving a gun in my face, enjoying watching me beg." He raised himself up until he was leaning forward, his one visible eye glittering with tears. "We need to be gone before he gets back."

Jace risked a glance at his brother. Arms still crossed over his chest, Eli looked to be in deep thought, but Jace knew better. There was uncertainty in the set of his face. They were caught up in something none of them had ever experienced and Eli was just as out of his depth as the rest of them.

"Where are the car keys?" Jace wanted to move things along. Get out of the house as quickly as possible and drop Felix off at the hospital, not because he feared Micky Blyte's return, but to untangle himself from the mess he'd landed them all in. What would Eli and Cat say if they knew he'd only seen Blyte once, exchanged less than a handful of words with the man?

He waited for Eli to respond but his brother stood unmoving like a tightly-bunched tree trunk.

"If it's not safe here, we should go." Jace tried again. He looked to Cat for support, hating himself for using her fear as a leverage to get Eli moving, but what choice did he have?

"He's right." Cat's eyes, startlingly green against her pale skin remained wide with fear. Jace wanted to put his arms around her. Tell her he'd keep her safe, but instead he looked down at his feet.

"You said he had a gun?" Eli continued with the questions as if no one had spoken.

"Yes, that's right." Even Felix's voice sounded stronger now. "That's one of the reasons we need to go." He shifted his body, one hand still pressed against his ribs. "I don't want to sound ungrateful, but we're wasting time. I can tell you whatever else you want to know in the car."

Eli nodded. Jace let out a breath. Once they were on the road, he could figure out a way of keeping the three of them out of trouble. He'd have to come clean about Blyte and the house, but the truth could wait until they dropped Felix at the hospital.

"Jace, Caitlin, we need to grab our stuff and go." Eli jerked his chin towards the door, indicating that he wanted the two of them to follow him.

Jace hesitated. As eager as he was to go, he felt uneasy about leaving Felix alone. He almost said something, but shrugged off the feeling as paranoia. He'd smoked weed and then found a man locked in the cellar, was it any wonder he felt jumpy?

He followed Cat and Eli out of the room and across the open-plan sitting room. His flip-flops slapped the stone floor, the sound noisy and conspicuous in the silent house. As they filed into the kitchen, Jace couldn't help snatching a glance behind him. For a split second, he thought he saw the study door move. He stopped walking and waited but the door remained a jar, just as he'd left it. *Jesus, this place is really getting to me.*

Once in the kitchen, Cat set about taking their stuff out of the fridge and putting the remaining cans on the counter. "Just leave that." Eli's voice was clipped, as if he were straining to keep himself under control.

Cat blinked and stopped moving. Jace could see a blush creeping up her slender neck. He wanted to say something. Tell his brother to stop being an asshole, but Cat looked close to tears, starting an argument with his brother would only make things worse. He clamped his lips together and leaned on the counter opposite the fridge.

"Something's really out of whack here." Eli stood with his hands on his hips as if addressing an audience. "Apart from the obvious, I get the feeling that guy's not telling us everything."

"So, what are you saying?" Jace couldn't hold his tongue any longer. He was sick of his brother ordering everyone around. It might have worked when they were teenagers, but Jace no longer saw his older brother as a hero.

"I'm saying, I don't want that guy... Felix, in the car with us. We should go, but leave him here. We can stop at the police station and send the cops to sort things out."

Jace opened his mouth to protest, but Cat spoke up first. "I found something upstairs in the linen cupboard." Both Jace and Eli turned in her direction. Her hands hung at her sides, bunched into fists as if she were bracing herself.

"Now's not the time." Eli sounded tired just by speaking.

Ignoring his dismissive attitude, she continued. "Wait here, I'll get it." She turned, hair fanning out behind her in a reddish-gold ribbons, and darted out of the kitchen.

"Why don't you pull your head in?" Jace had promised himself he wouldn't interfere. With everything else that was going on, he knew it was a mistake to say anything, but the way Eli was treating Cat made him want to strangle his brother.

"What are you talking about?" Everything about the way Eli spoke told his brother he knew exactly what he was talking about.

"What has she done that's so wrong?" He held up his hand. "You know what, don't bother. You're a fucking hypocrite and you know it."

Eli took a step forward. His eyes narrowed until they were little more than slits. Jace had seen this look before, it usually signalled trouble. When they were kids, Eli always got real quiet just before he struck out. By the time Jace was eight, he knew to watch for those narrow eyes and learned when to run. But things had changed, Jace wasn't afraid of his older brother anymore and judging by the way Eli hesitated, he knew it too.

The silence screamed with tension. Jace could hear his own breathing, louder than a cannon in his ears. If he were honest with himself, he'd like a physical confrontation with his brother. As much as he'd idolised him at one time in his life, he was hungry for the chance to show him he wasn't so big and bad anymore.

"Look at this." Cat trotted back into the room holding a silver box which she set down on the bench top. The metal hit the marble with a *ding*.

As if sensing trouble, she stopped moving and looked from Jace to Eli. "Has something happened?"

Eli circled his shoulders as if limbering up for a fight. "It's nothing, just my little brother being a twerp." He smiled at his wife, a tight-lipped forced lift of the corners of his mouth. It wasn't the smile that really got to Jace, but Cat's reaction. Her lips parted and a puff of breath escaped. It was a small movement, but he could see how relieved she was to be thrown such a small scrap of approval. In that moment, he disliked his brother with almost as much depth as he'd once loved him.

He'd planned this weekend in the hopes of helping Cat and Eli put the pieces of their fractured relationship back together. At least that's what he'd told himself, but now he knew it was Cat he'd been trying to help, not Eli. His love for his brother had leaked away like water out of a cracked glass.

The catches on the side of the box clicked open, snapping him back to the moment. "Look." Cat opened the lid and turned the box so Jace and Eli could see its contents.

"Shit." The word whistled out of Eli's mouth in a tone that sounded more like admiration than surprise. "Felix said Blyte waved a gun in his face, this must be it." He pulled the box across the benchtop until it was sitting in front of him. "Where did you say you found it?" He spoke with his eyes on the gun.

"It was in the linen cupboard, hidden at the bottom." Cat pursed her lips as if in thought. Jace found himself wondering what it would be like to feel those lips on his neck. It was a fleeting but dangerous thought. He turned his attention back to the gun avoiding making eye contact with his sister-in-law.

"This doesn't change anything." Eli pointed at the box. "I still think we should leave Felix here and send help."

When the repercussions of what Eli was suggesting sunk in, Jace's heart thumped with panic. His brother wanted to go to the cops and tell them about Felix. If they did, Jace would be in trouble up to his eyeballs. He had to find a way to convince Eli and Cat that it would be better to go along with Felix's idea and drop the guy off at the hospital.

He searched for some line of reasoning, anything to make the second option more appealing, but he came up blank. He placed his hands on the island bench, icy under his palms. "Let's just think this through." He tapped the side of the box. "This changes things. Whatever Blyte's doing with Felix is one thing." Jace shrugged. "Assault, maybe kidnapping, but the handgun makes it more serious."

"So what are you saying?" Cat asked.

He opened his mouth, but a distant sound caught his attention. Within seconds, he could see the other two heard it too. He looked into Cat's green eyes. Huge and shiny with fear, they reminded him of an injured bird's. A knot of dread twisted in his gut.

Eli reached forward and picked up the gun.

Chapter Five

Hearing a sound and really registering it are two different things. It took Caitlin almost two full seconds between registering a distant noise and understanding what it was. An engine, the hiss of tyres on gravel. The saliva dried in her mouth leaving her tongue dry like a day-old waffle. There was no mistaking the sound of a car approaching. *He's dangerous*, Felix's words bounced around her mind. He'd warned them. *We should have gone while we had the chance.* If it hadn't been for Eli they'd be on the road now, headed towards Mandurah.

She watched her husband pick up the gun. Part of her couldn't believe her eyes. This was supposed to be a fun weekend. A chance to get close to each other again. Now Eli had a gun in his hand and her knees trembled so badly she thought they might actually start knocking together like a cartoon character.

"What are you going to do?" Even as she asked the question, she could see the set of her husband's mouth, a hard line almost turned down at the edges. He meant to do something drastic. For some reason, she found herself turning to Jace for reassurance. "We can't go out there."

Jace took hold of her elbow, his fingers felt rigid against her skin as if he were handling explosives and wanted to make the least possible contact.

"Stay here." He moved around her, blocking the archway that led to the main room.

Her mouth opened, she wanted to argue and protest, but from the front of the house came the sound of a car door slamming. Jace let go of her arm.

"I won't let anything happen," his voice was soft. "It'll be okay."

She watched them file out of the room, Eli in the lead with Jace following. Caitlin stepped back, pressing her spine against the island bench, grateful for something solid to lean on. The only sound came from Jace's flip-flops slapping across the stone floor. A minute or so later, a scrape as something large was moved or dragged. Then voices.

Caitlin stepped up to the archway. She heard Eli's, loud and commanding. He and Jace stood near the main entrance, a heavy looking dark wood cabinet had been wedged against the front door.

"Don't try to come in, I've got your gun."

She couldn't hear whoever Eli addressed, but judging by the way he leaned towards the door, someone spoke from the outside.

"Get in your car and drive away. We're leaving and taking Felix with us." His voice sounded uncertain. She wondered what Blyte, if that was who was out there, was saying.

Cowering in the background struck her as ridiculous. She wanted to know what was happening. Whatever was being decided affected her as much as everyone else. Eli had the gun and the door was barricaded, Blyte couldn't get in. *Now all I have to do is force my rubbery legs to move.*

Taking the first step was the hardest part. When her foot came down on the floor, it wobbled as if it might slide out from under her. But her legs held and she managed to make it across the room. On the way, she glanced towards the study. Felix had to be able to hear what was going on. Why hadn't he come out? *Maybe he's like me, shaking with fear.* After what he'd been through, she couldn't blame him. Another possibility might be that he couldn't walk unaided. He'd needed Eli and Jace to help him into the study.

"I can't let you take him." The voice, muffled but audible, came from the other side of the door.

From her position behind Jace, Caitlin guessed Blyte had to be standing close to the front door. Eli held the gun up, pointed straight ahead as if ready to shoot. Was it loaded? She couldn't remember if he picked up the clip or just the gun. Did he even know how to load a gun? The questions tumbled through her mind. She considered asking Jace, but decided against it.

"I don't care about you *or* what you're doing in my house." Caitlin jumped. The disembodied voice was louder as if the man were pressed against the door. "Whatever he's told you is lies. This is between me and him."

He didn't sound crazy but she supposed they never did. Just looking at the house told her he was successful. He had to be able to get along in the world without anyone knowing what was going on in his head. Maybe he was just good at convincing people to believe him.

Eli looked over his shoulder, catching her eye. She could see a film of sweat forming on his forehead, clinging to his dark hair. He looked uncertain, his gazed darted away as if he knew she'd caught the look.

"Get away from the door," Eli raised his voice to match the one coming from the other side. He paused, his breathing loud in the silence. "I'm not fucking around. If I have to, I'll shoot."

Caitlin sucked in a breath. She didn't like the edge in her husband's voice, it sounded alien, almost crackling with desperation. She looked to Jace but his gaze remained locked on the door. The seconds ticked by without a response from Blyte. She wondered if he'd gone back to his car. Maybe he'd leave, just drive away into the night. Was it possible Eli's threats had worked?

The silence stretched. If Blyte intended to leave, they'd have heard his car start. Caitlin tried to remember what the front of the house looked like when they arrived. The driveway was a long, curved, strip of red pea gravel, if he *was* walking back to his car, surely they'd hear his shoes crunching over the loose stones.

"The back door." When she managed to get the words out, they bounced off the walls and echoed in the cavernous house.

Jace reacted first, running past her so fast, she felt a rush of air against her bare arm. He dodged the oversized sofa and disappeared into the kitchen with Eli on his tail. She stood rooted to the spot, listening to their raised voices and hurried movements. Next came grunting and scraping. She guessed they were dragging something across the back door, most likely the fridge.

By blocking both the exits, they were preventing Blyte from getting in, but what if they needed to get out in a hurry? For all they knew, the man outside might decide to set the house on fire. Caitlin ran her fingers through her hair and looked around. The windows were so narrow and high in the walls, it would be difficult to climb out. They'd be trapped, overcome by smoke before they made it outside.

The thoughts bubbled in her mind, boiling and churning. She had to calm herself or she'd lose control and start shrieking. The situation was strange, volatile even, but no one had been hurt. *What about Felix?* Her brain threw up an image of him slumped on the cellar floor, bruised and dirty. Blyte did that to him. If he was capable of torturing someone, who knew what he'd do if they pushed him.

A bang, sudden and heavy shook the front door. Caitlin screamed and stepped back as the solid wooden door shuddered under the weight of the blow.

"We should have gone when we had the chance." Felix spoke from behind her.

She let out another scream and spun to the right, off-balance and stumbling. A hand grabbed her arm, pulling her back as she tried to run.

"Let go," her voice high and shrill with fear. The room blurred for a second, only coming back into focus in bursts of light and colour.

"I'm sorry. I didn't mean to scare you." Felix let go of her arm and shuffled back a few steps. "I heard the voices and banging... I came to help." He leaned against the wall breathing heavily.

"What's going on?" Eli appeared next to her. His face and bare chest were shiny with sweat, from heavy lifting. The gun dangled loosely from his hand.

Before she could answer, the door shuddered as if hit by something weighty. Caitlin took hold of the hem of her dress, balling her hands into tight fists. No one moved. Felix and Eli stared at the door.

"Give me the gun." When Felix spoke, she saw her husband's shoulders jerk as if he were startled. *He's as scared as me.* The thought only fuelled her own terror. If Eli, always strong and sure of himself, was frightened, then the danger was all the more real.

"He won't go. He'll never let us leave." He reached out his hand. "We have to stop him." Felix's voice shook. Caitlin wondered if it was fear or anger affecting the man. He'd obviously been through hell. It made sense he was frightened, and holding the gun would give him back some semblance of power.

"What are you planning to do?" Eli sounded calmer than he looked. Judging by his tone of voice, he was actually contemplating giving the gun to Felix.

"I'm going to shoot him." The tremor had left Felix's voice. The words were still slushy over his swollen lip, but he sounded confident—resigned. Eli hesitated. "It's the only way."

To Caitlin's astonishment, her husband nodded. He lifted his hand as if ready to turn over the weapon. Caitlin sprang forward and grabbed Eli's wrist.

"No. You can't." She tried to look into her husband's eyes but his gaze was fixed on the floor. "Eli." When he finally looked up, his pupils were huge, his eyes watery. "We can't let him shoot a man. It's murder."

"It's self-defence," Felix spoke from behind her.

Ignoring him, she kept talking. "We don't know anything about what's happening here, but if you give him the gun, then you're part of whatever happens next." She tightened her grip on his wrist, the tendons felt bunched and tight. "Just take time to think this over."

He nodded, this time with more conviction. She felt the muscles in his wrist relax.

"Okay." He looked past her and spoke to Felix. "I think you should go back in the study."

"This is insane," Felix's voice was high with disbelief. "You don't get it, do you? We're all going to die if—"

"Get in the study." Jace's shoulders almost filled the wide archway. He looked different, threatening and immovable. She'd been so fixated on Eli and the gun, she hadn't heard him approach.

Felix looked like he was about to argue, but another look at Jace changed his mind. His shoulders slumped and he let out a huff of air. No one spoke, the only sound came from Felix's slow departure. Feet shuffling and one hand on the wall for support, he made his way back to the study.

* * *

Blyte backed away from the door and let the shadows close over him. There were others in his house, at least two. He'd heard a woman's voice, faint but distinct. He pulled out a pack of cigarettes and jammed one between his lips. Leaving Felix had been a mistake and now there were others involved. If they'd found one of his guns, things could get messy.

Even if they turned on the outside lights, they'd never get a clear shot at him, the angles were all wrong. They'd have to come outside. Once they were out in the open, he had no doubt he could disarm the man. But what then?

He took a drag on the cigarette, the glowing end momentarily illuminating his battered knuckles. He could walk away, let them leave, but that would mean giving up everything. *No*, this was his only chance. It didn't matter how the others ended up in his house, they were involved now and he wasn't about to let them go. *Not until I'm finished with Felix.* He tossed the butt onto the dirt and ground it out with his boot. They'd come out or he'd get in, either way no one was leaving.

* * *

There'd been no sound from outside the house in almost ten minutes. Caitlin wanted to believe Blyte had given up and left, but while there'd been no banging, they hadn't heard his car start up either. He was out there somewhere. The thought gave her chills.

"We could wait until morning, he might give up and leave," she tried to sound convincing.

They were in the main room. After Felix returned to the study, Jace closed the door behind him giving them some privacy. The temperature hadn't dropped. If anything, Caitlin felt hotter. Or maybe it was the tension simmering in the air that made the house seem stuffy and oppressive.

"You know Blyte," Eli turned to his brother as if she hadn't spoken. "Could this be a drug deal gone wrong?" He nodded to the gun now sitting on the coffee table next to a tarnished candlestick. "It would explain the gun."

Perched on the arm of the sofa to Caitlin's left, Jace shifted his weight. A large V-shaped patch of sweat had formed on the front of his t-shirt. They were all tense, on edge, but Jace seemed jittery.

"I don't know Blyte." His head hung down as if he were contemplating something on his hands. He spoke without looking up. "I did some work for him a few months ago, that's how I knew the house would be empty this week." He rubbed the back of his neck. "Or at least that's what I heard him tell one of the other tradesmen."

"I don't understand." Caitlin couldn't believe what she was hearing. She'd always thought of Jace as a bit of a larrikin but not a liar. "You said he was a mate."

"I don't believe this." Eli jumped to his feet and stood over his brother. "If you don't know the guy then how come you have the keys?"

Jace let out a breath. "I—He left a house key for me and the boss. We needed to get the deck out back finished so we wanted to start earlier than the other tradies. Blyte gave my boss, Rick, the key. Rick took off early one afternoon and gave me the key so I could lock up before I left." He raised his head and spoke directly to his brother. "I heard Blyte telling the electrician he'd be out of the country for the whole of January, so I had the key copied."

Caitlin felt a crawling sensation in the pit of her stomach as if something slithered around inside her. She wanted to get out of the house, breathe the night air and put some distance between herself and the isolated building.

"What the hell were you thinking?" Eli's voice was almost a roar. He took a step and was on top of Jace, looking down on him. "Do you realise what you've done?" He grabbed the front of Jace's t-shirt and tried to pull him to his feet.

The sound of fabric tearing got Caitlin moving. She stood and took hold of Eli's left arm, trying to pull him off his brother. At the same time Jace shoved Eli in the chest and he stumbled back, pulling her with him. The back of his legs hit the coffee table sending it sliding out from behind him and him careening onto the stone floor. Before she could get her balance, Caitlin fell with him, her right knee taking the impact as she hit the floor.

She cried out in shock more than pain and rolled to the side clutching her injured knee. Eli, on the floor beside her reached out to her, but Jace beat him to it.

"Sorry, Cat. Are you okay?" Jace took hold of her upper arm and helped her stand.

"I'm fine, just bumped my knee." There were tears in her eyes, both from the injury and because of the flare up between the brothers. She'd never seen them so aggressive with each other. It was as if everything was coming undone, including her marriage.

"That's why you got us here." Eli scrambled to his feet. "Because of her." He pointed an accusing finger in Caitlin's direction, kept his gaze on his brother. "What? Did you think she'd realise what an asshole I am and fall into bed with you?"

Caitlin couldn't believe what she was hearing. One minute they were talking about Blyte and the mess they were in, and suddenly Eli was accusing Jace of trying to get her into bed. She opened her mouth to protest but couldn't find the words.

The colour drained out of Jace's face. "How can you even think that?" His voice was hoarse as if the words stuck in his throat. "I did all this to try and give you two a chance to patch things up."

Still bare-chested and glistening with sweat, Eli tilted his head back and laughed. There was no humour in the sound. "Don't worry, mate. You can have her."

Caitlin winced as if he slapped her. His words dripped with disgust. *Does he really hate me that much?* She flopped down onto the couch, the tears flowing. She didn't bother to try and hide them. He'd been cold and distant for months. She knew he blamed her for losing the baby. God knows she blamed herself, but she had no idea his feelings were so dark. She only wished she knew where this level of hatred came from.

No sooner than the question formed in her mind, Eli answer it. "I know all about the abortion." He turned to her, making eye contact for the first time since the altercation between him and Jace began. His face was screwed up and tears glistened in his dark eyes. "I heard you at the hospital."

Caitlin covered her ears with her hands trying to block out what he was saying, but it was no good. She couldn't hide from the truth by pushing the memories away. She'd spent a lifetime shoving the past into a dark hole but no matter what she did, they still kept crawling out.

"Stop it." Jace moved in front of her, blocking Eli.

"No." Eli's voice bounced off the walls. "You were there." He jabbed a finger into his brother's chest. "You heard her telling the doctor. She had an abortion at fifteen. Fifteen." He gave another hollow laugh. "I thought she was perfect. The perfect woman, but she's just a slut. And that's why the baby—"

Jace struck out. His fist connected with Eli's cheek, with a dull thud. The blow couldn't have been hard, Eli barely moved, but the shock on his face was as clear as the red welt spreading across his skin. He pushed his younger brother without any real force and stormed towards the kitchen. But not before Caitlin caught a glimpse of his tortured expression.

"Eli, I'm sorry," Jace called after him, but Eli kept moving.

She expected Jace to go after him but instead, he dropped down next to her on the sofa. She got a faint whiff of weed mingled with aftershave. He lowered his head into his hands, fingers laced through messy blond hair. He looked defeated.

"How long have you known?" Even talking about the abortion made her feel naked—exposed in some way. It was as if all the pain and loathing were laid bare for everyone to see, yet she had to know.

He didn't answer right away. For a moment, she thought he wasn't going to and then he spoke, his voice barely audible. "Since that day at the hospital. Eli was with me when he got the call." He paused as if drawing enough breath to finish what he had to say. "I drove. I didn't want him to have to go alone. When we got to your room, we could hear you talking to the doctor…"

"Oh." Caitlin drew her legs up under her, feeling the pain in her knee but not reacting. So now she knew why her husband blamed her for losing the baby. He was right to blame her. It was her fault. The doctor even confirmed that the complications after the abortion could make it difficult for her to carry a baby to term. Somehow, it was easier to accept her husband's loathing in the face of what he knew about her.

In spite of the heat, she felt a cold chill on her skin. The tears had dried up leaving a strained tautness in her throat. It was over, her marriage and any hopes of a happy family all at an end. There should have been more pain, but all she felt was empty.

"I'm sorry, Cat." Jace was looking at her now, she could see the pity in his eyes. "He didn't mean it. You know what he's like."

She was about to speak, tell him they both knew what Eli was like when the banging started again. Jace stood and grabbed the gun from the coffee table. As he passed the study, the door cracked open. She couldn't see Felix from her position on the couch, but she saw Jace stop and heard him tell the man to get back in the room. The anger in his voice didn't surprise her. She guessed his nerves were raw.

Another thundering blow rang out from the door. The heavy, ominous sound made her skin prick with chills. She thought of a line from a poem she'd once read: *Send not to know for whom the bell tolls, it tolls for thee.* She couldn't remember the poet's name, but the heavy repetitive boom made her think of a funeral bell.

Jace approached the door and leaned over the hulking dark wood cabinet blocking the entrance, pressing the tips of his fingers against the wood. In his other hand, the gun hung, its barrel pointing at the floor.

"Listen." Jace raised his voice trying to be heard over the thumping from the other side of the door. "We don't care what happened between you and Felix, it's none of our business."

The pounding stopped. Caitlin rushed towards the door and stood behind Jace. They waited, the absence of sound almost more threatening than the banging.

"You're right." Blyte's voice came from outside. "It's none of your business." He sounded breathless. "Open the door. You and whoever's in there can just get in your car and leave. No one has to get hurt."

Jace glanced at her, she wondered if he was looking for answers. If only she knew what to do, how to make it all stop, but there was no easy way out.

"Ask about Felix." She kept her voice low, barely above a whisper.

Jace nodded. "What about Felix?"

"Don't trust him." The three words hung in the air like dark clouds, unpredictable and threatening.

Caitlin recalled her earlier doubts about barricading themselves in; she'd been worried about what Blyte might do.

"Get Eli," Jace kept his voice low and jerked his head towards the kitchen.

For the three years they'd been married and the eighteen months they'd dated, Caitlin remembered feeling excited at the prospect of sharing some new nugget of information with her husband. She treasured the time they spent laughing about the strangeness of the world or chatting about something she'd seen on the news. Now, the thought of talking to him invoked dread.

57

Without speaking, she turned and trotted to the kitchen. With each step anxiety built. By the time she walked through the arch, her stomach had clenched itself into a tight ball.

Eli sat on the island bench, head in hands. She fleetingly wondered why he wasn't using one of the three black stools wedged under the bench. Caitlin knew he'd heard the banging at the front door, there was no way he could have missed it, even in the kitchen. Whatever he thought of her, how could he ignore what was happening around them? For the first time since she'd met him, it occurred to her that maybe he wasn't as strong and capable as he seemed.

He raised his head before she had the chance to speak. His eyes were red-rimmed as if he'd been crying. He turned away, studying something on the cellar door. The things he'd said hurt, made her feel dirty and worthless, but she couldn't ignore the pain in his eyes. If only there was something she could say or do to put everything right.

"You'd better come, we need your help."

"I'm sure you and Jace can manage." He sounded bitter, almost childish.

"Whatever you think of me doesn't matter. For your brother's sake *and* your own, stop crying and help us." She was surprised at the strength in her voice and wondered where it came from. Desperation?

Eli's head snapped around so he was finally facing her. He blinked as if not sure of what he saw, then rubbed his eyes with the heels of his hands and jumped off the bench. Grateful her words had at least penetrated his temper, she turned and walked back to the front of the house. Behind her, Eli's bare feet smacked the floor.

Jace was still holding the gun facing the door. When they approached, he turned and glanced at his brother.

"You okay?" He sounded calm.

"Yep." Eli's response, although curt, no longer carried any threat of anger.

Jace turned his attention back to Blyte. "We just want to take Felix to the hospital. That's all. No one's talking about the police, if that's what you're worried about."

Blyte gave a scoffing laugh. "Yes, the police. They'd want to know what you were doing in my house." His voice was deep, almost raspy. Caitlin wished she could see the man because in her mind, he was a giant. A big dark man with burning eyes.

Blyte continued, "Was it Felix's idea to go to the hospital instead of the police?"

It *had* been Felix's idea. Caitlin remembered he suggested they drop him off at the hospital and he would have the doctors contact the police. A strange suggestion now she came to think of it. But then again, he'd been abducted and tortured, was it any surprise that he might say or do something odd?

"We should just open the door and go out," Eli spoke in a whisper, he jerked his chin towards his brother. "You've got the gun. There's two of us and one of him, what's he going to do?"

"What if *he* has a gun?" Caitlin pointed at the weapon in Jace's hand. "He had that one hidden upstairs, what if he has more?"

She could see by the looks on Jace and Eli's faces, it hadn't occurred to them that Blyte might be carrying a gun. If the windows weren't so high up in the walls, she could take a look. At least then they'd know what they were dealing with.

She made a rolling motion with her hand. *Keep him talking*, she mouthed the words.

Jace frowned but nodded. "What is it with you and Felix? Drugs?"

Caitlin knew she'd probably have a better chance of seeing Blyte from one of the upstairs windows, but the thought of venturing off into the cavernous house alone made her nervous. Besides, she wanted to hear what was being said.

Turning in a circle, she settled on the coffee table but quickly changed her mind and headed for the kitchen. A stool would offer height and be easier to lift, not nearly as noisy as dragging the small table.

In the seconds it took to dash through to the kitchen and return with the stool, she could see something had happened. There was a change in the two brothers' demeanour, subtle but nonetheless disturbing.

Instead of asking what had happened, she carried the stool to the window on the far right of the door and set it down. Whatever was going on, she still wanted to get a look at Blyte.

"What do you mean, Felix is a murderer? If that's true, why did you bring him here? Why not go to the cops?"

Eli's words took her by surprise. One knee on the stool, Caitlin froze and turned back to the brothers. The two men leaned closer to the door, waiting for answers. She snatched a look over her shoulder and was relieved to see the study door remained closed. *Can he hear us*? She wondered if Felix was listening to the conversation, maybe pressed up against the door.

Still half on the stool, she checked her watch. Almost ten o'clock, it had been less than half an hour since Blyte arrived, yet it seemed like they'd been living out this nightmare for hours.

"The police had their chance to put him away and did nothing." Blyte stopped. For a moment, she thought he was finished. "Now it's my turn."

"So you brought him here." Now it was Jace asking the questions. "To do what? Beat him to death?"

Caitlin pushed herself up onto the stool, crouching at first to get her balance. Then, using the wall for support, she straightened up. Standing at full height, her head and shoulders were above the window ledge. The world beyond the house was a black expanse cut through by shadowy treetops that danced against the night sky.

She cupped her hands and pressed them to the window. The glass felt like ice against her skin. Caitlin shivered and leaned closer so her nose almost touched the pane. To the left, she could make out a shape. With no outside light, it was difficult to tell if the dark outline belonged to a bush or a human. The shape moved and what looked like the outline of an arm appeared.

"No." Blyte was either a good actor or he was shocked by the suggestion. "I'm not a killer. I brought him here for answers."

She shuffled sideways, the stool tipped slightly. Caitlin let out a gasp and clutched the window ledge. Eli and Jace turned in her direction. From her vantage point on the stool, their upturned faces looked pale and anxious. She held up a hand to let them know she was okay and pressed her face back to the window.

The angle was a little better. She could see more of Blyte's shape, but without light, it was almost impossible to tell if he had a weapon.

"So you abducted a man and locked him in the cellar because you wanted answers?" This time Eli spoke. It was as if the brothers were taking turns.

She pulled back from the window. There had to be outside lights, if they turned them on, she'd be able to get a clear look at Blyte and then they'd have a better picture of what they were dealing with.

To her surprise, Jace had left the door and was standing below her. "Can you tell where he's parked his car?" he spoke in a whisper. "See if he's blocked Eli in."

"We should turn on the lights," she matched his whisper.

"Not yet."

She nodded. It might be better to leave them off until they decided what to do. The darkness was more of a disadvantage to Blyte. With her hands back on the pane, she squinted into the blackness. Beyond the front of the house, lay dark shapes, some large, others smaller. It took a minute for her eyes to adjust to the darkness and for the hulking shapes of the two vehicles to come into focus.

On the left, a smaller shape that had to be Eli's compact Mazda. Parked off to the right, a larger vehicle. Only it's outline visible under the moonless sky, but it was clearly parked alongside Eli's car.

Caitlin pulled back from the window. "No. Eli's car's clear."

Jace offered her his hand. She hesitated for a second, remembering what Eli said about his brother wanting to get her into bed. Her husband's words stung, but if she were truthful with herself, she'd always been attracted to Jace. He was good looking and athletic, but more importantly kind and easy-going. It was a vague attraction, nothing she'd ever dream of acting on. How could she when all her energy went into pleasing Eli? Besides, Jace had never been anything but brotherly with her.

She took his hand and leaped down from the stool. Jace let go of her fingers and motioned for Eli to join them in the kitchen. Eli held up his hand, a sign he wanted them to wait.

"What answers?" he turned his attention back to the door.

"Ask him about Amy."

Chapter Six

"We should have tried to find out more about the woman, Amy," Eli's voice was low. "If this is over a woman, it might be better to just let them sort it out."

The three of them had retreated to the kitchen and stood around the island bench. It had been Jace's idea to talk where they could be sure neither Felix nor Blyte could hear them.

"So you think we should leave Felix and go?" Jace sounded surprised. "You saw what Blyte did to him."

Eli dragged his forearm over his face, wiping away a layer of sweat. "Whatever's going on between Blyte and Felix, it's none of our business." He looked at Caitlin, only making eye contact for the briefest of seconds before turning back to his brother. "I say we go and let the cops come back and sort it out."

"I don't know." Caitlin didn't want to make the problem worse by provoking another outburst from Eli, but she couldn't stay silent. "Blyte could have a gun. Once we're outside the house anything could happen."

Eli tipped his head back, eyes on the ceiling as if searching for patience from above. Usually, her husband's obvious annoyance would be enough to silence her. But not this time. She'd been tearing herself for months trying to figure out what she'd done to drive him away. Now the secret was out; both hers and his. He knew about the abortion but instead of talking to her about it, he'd punished her for months with cold disdain. Maybe she was guilty, but so was he.

"The three of us trying to get to the car is a bad idea." The words were out. Like it or not, she'd spoken her mind.

"I agree." Jace didn't give Eli time to argue. "I'll go alone. I can get out through the back door and sneak around to the car while you keep him talking." He nodded to his brother then turned to Caitlin. "You keep an eye on him from the window."

"And if he has a gun?" Caitlin didn't want to think what might happen, but she had to ask.

"We'll make sure we distract Blyte long enough for me to get in the car and get going." He sounded confident, sure of what he was saying. They listened to Jace's plan, but as he spoke, Caitlin found herself staring at the fridge. The huge appliance was wedged against the back door. Wrenched from the socket, its long power cable lay on the floor. Dragging the fridge had left gouge marks in the stone floor.

"How are we going to get that thing back in place once you leave?" Eli and Jace looked at the fridge, it had obviously been a struggle for the two men to move it.

"Shit." Jace's shoulders slumped.

"We'll manage." Eli shrugged. "If we can't shift it, we'll get Felix to help."

With everyone in agreement, there was nothing left to discuss. Caitlin volunteered to go upstairs and retrieve the car keys from their travel bag.

She left the brothers in the kitchen and headed through the sitting room. As she made her way towards the staircase, she recalled her first impressions of the house. She'd been so impressed by its vastness and the wealth it represented, now the oversized rooms and high ceilings gave her the creeps. She felt vulnerable and exposed in the rambling structure. There were so many places to hide, so much space to cover. Anyone could be lurking in the house and they'd never know it. *We spent all afternoon here and most of the evening before we realised someone was locked in the cellar.*

Taking the stairs two at a time, she hurried up to the landing. The upstairs lights illuminated the long expanse well enough for her to find their room, but not enough to chase all the shadows away. She paused on her way along the L-shaped walkway and listened. This far from the kitchen, she could hear nothing but the distant clicking of insects and a faint but regular cry of an owl. The sounds might have been comforting, but instead reminded her of how far away from the city they were.

Once in the bedroom, she knelt on the soft grey carpet and pulled the travel bag towards her. There was no need to search, the keys were safely stowed in the side compartment. For once, Eli's attention to detail and habit seemed less annoying. Placing the keys in her lap, Caitlin took hold of the zip when an idea struck.

Instead of closing the zip, she reached into the pocket and found her husband's phone. She'd read somewhere that it was possible to send a text message even if the signal was weak. If it worked, she could send their address and a request for help to emergency services. Her stomach flipped with a tiny flutter of excitement. The prospect of getting help and escaping from the house before anyone got hurt made her realise how terrified she'd become.

Unlocking the phone was easy, Eli's password was the same as his pin number. The green bar on the top right of the screen told her the phone was almost fully charged. She whispered a thank you to the empty room and typed in *000*. It would be best, she decided to keep the message short.

Attacked by man with gun. Need help.

She followed up with the address and hit send. Almost as quickly as her hopes rose, they were dashed. The message failed to send. Caitlin sank onto her butt and crossed her legs. She heaved a sigh that came from deep in the pit of her belly and willed herself not to cry. Jace and Eli were waiting for her. There would be no talking them out of the plan. Jace would go outside and take his chances with Blyte. In theory, it was a sound idea—the only idea they had. But a creeping feeling of dread spread over her and with it came a flat certainty that something would go wrong.

The phone was useless, help wasn't coming. She reached out and almost put the phone back where she'd found it when Eli's words popped into her mind. He'd called her a slut. If she hadn't heard it with her own ears, she wouldn't have believed he was capable of saying such a thing. Not about her.

For months he'd been distant, almost contemptuous. She'd had no idea what he knew about her and how that knowledge had twisted his feelings. What else was he hiding? *Do I want to know?* That was the problem with secrets, once they were out, there was no turning back.

She almost shoved the phone back in the side compartment, but a small voice in her head, whispered. *If he hasn't touched me since before I lost the baby, who has he been touching?* She opened his messages and didn't even have to scroll through them to find the answer.

Can't wait for you to get back. Miss you already. XXX

The message was from someone named Sherri. Caitlin stared at the words as if they might jump around on the screen, morph into something that didn't set her teeth on edge. She scrolled through and read Eli's response to Sherri.

When I get back, we'll go out for dinner. Somewhere nice. I'm picturing you in that red dress! You look otherworldly!!! Driving me crazy. XXX

Her hands shook making it difficult to swipe the screen. There were other messages. Some she'd sent herself asking Eli if he was going to be home late again or reminding him to pick her up from work because her car was being serviced. In each instant, her mundane message was rewarded with little more than a one-word answer: *yes, no,* or *okay.* But so many words for Sherri.

Otherworldly. The word reverberated in her brain like a bullet ricocheting in a metal cylinder. She stuffed the phone back in the bag and pulled the zip closed. How had she been so unseeing? So weak? The urge to crawl into the unmade bed and draw pain around herself surfaced. What did it matter if they were prisoners in this house? She'd be a prisoner wherever she went. This feeling, self-loathing mixed with betrayal and grief, was now her future. Why bother fighting for it?

Her hand dropped to her belly. *I couldn't even get that right.* Could she really blame Eli for going elsewhere? Maybe Sherri, whoever she was, gave him things Caitlin never could. Was he planning a future with the woman? For some reason, her mother's face jumped into her mind. Once pretty, her features blurred and bloated by alcohol and bitterness. *All men are bastards, even the nice ones.* How many times had she heard those words coming out of her mother's mouth?

The air in the bedroom tasted thick, difficult to swallow. Caitlin ran her hands over her face, stretching the skin as she pushed her head through a layer of painful memories. She recalled something else her mother once said. Speech slurred, barely making sense but still able to hold a glass, Linda Blackson was never one to know when enough was enough. Not when it came to alcohol or men. If she did, she never let it stop her.

"I was like you." Linda's watery blue eyes had fixed on Caitlin then bobbed drunkenly with the effort of focusing. "Sweet." She'd laughed then coughed, a rattling smoker's hack. "Sweet attracts sour." She swept her arm wide, almost spilling her drink. "That's why I'm in this shit hole." Caitlin wasn't sure if she meant the dingy two-bedroom rental on the edge of town or the town itself. Both were falling apart and neglected.

"I lost myself." Her mother flopped down next to her on the sagging sofa. "I never knew how to claw my way back so I just kept falling." The smell of cigarettes mixed with whiskey had made Caitlin's stomach churn. "Don't be like me. Be the woman I should have been." She patted Caitlin's bare knee. "You're smart, but you keep it quiet. You show them what you can do."

Her hand slipped off Caitlin's knee. Within seconds, her mother's breathing had deepened. Caitlin leaned over and took the glass out of Linda's hand. By the time she set it on the side table, her mother was snoring.

Caitlin looked around the bedroom with its expensive furnishings and plush carpet. Eli's clothing, stacked neatly on top of the chest of drawers stirred something in her. She stood and swiped his belongs onto the floor. It was a petty thing to do but it gave her a second of satisfaction. She thought of the way she'd clung to Eli, turning herself inside out to please him. Not just in the last few months but for most of their marriage. She'd let him become her entire world, giving up her own wants and needs to please him. Her mother was right about one thing, they *were* alike. Both lost, living half-lives dependent on men to fulfil them.

Caitlin held the keys to her chest and opened the bedroom door. The pain and shock of betrayal still stung, like an open welt submerged in vinegar. But, instead of sinking under the misery of betrayal, Caitlin intended to claw her way out. Out of the mess her marriage had become *and* out of Blyte's house.

She was half-way to the staircase, mind racing with images of her husband's body pressed against another woman, when she realised someone was on the landing.

Her heart jumped and the keys tumbled from her hand, jingling then landing with a muted *clunk* on the carpet.

"Sorry. I didn't mean to startle you." Felix's frame blocked the walkway, face half in shadow.

Off balance by his sudden appearance, Caitlin found herself unable to speak. For a moment, there was silence.

"I—What are you doing?" The question came out sounding shrill, almost panicked. "I mean, why are you up here?" She tried to calm herself but her voice shook.

"I'm looking for the toilet." His tone was apologetic or was it amused? His swollen mouth made it difficult to tell.

"There's a powder room behind the staircase on the ground floor."

"Oh." She waited for him to turn and walk towards the staircase, but he remained rooted to the spot. "What are you doing with those keys?" His head moved, but she couldn't quite see his face.

Caitlin looked down at her hand, confused by his question. Then realising he meant the car keys, she gave an awkward laugh. "We…" She hesitated, not sure if she should be sharing their plans with him. Remembering Blyte's words, she asked her own question. "Who's Amy?"

He showed no signs of reacting to the name. "I don't know. Why do you ask?" Again, he managed to put her on the spot.

She wanted to be done with the conversation but didn't know how to extricate herself from the situation without being out-right rude. "Just a name I heard." She tossed the keys and then caught them. "I've got to go, my husband's waiting for me."

She stepped forward, expecting Felix to either turn and head down stairs or step aside. He did neither, forcing her to shuffle past him brushing against his arm. The smell she'd originally noticed in the study, earthy and laced with something metallic hit her again, only this time closer and more pungent. A snapshot flashed through her mind.

Sunlight through a car window, girlish voices singing. The image almost swamped her.

Memories swirled, fuelled by the smell, familiar and alien at the same time. Still reeling from the shock of discovering her husband's deceit, Caitlin couldn't afford to let the dark thoughts surface.

"Excuse me," she made her voice calm but firm and strode past Felix.

Once on the stairs, she felt a small measure of control return. *Be the woman I should have been.* She focused on her mother's words. Her knees shook. But for her firm grip on the banister, she might have taken a tumble. Whatever happened, she wouldn't allow herself to be paralysed by the past.

* * *

Jace held the poker he'd used to break the lock in the cellar. The brothers had pushed the fridge back from the door allowing just enough room for Jace to squeeze through and out onto the deck.

"Okay," Jace's voice was sombre, but his eyes were wide and the sweat patches on his shirt had grown. There was a tear along the neckline where Eli had grabbed him. "You both know what to do, right?"

Caitlin nodded, she couldn't bring herself to look at her husband.

"If anything goes wrong, I'll make for the trees and circle back around when it's safe."

"Maybe you should take the gun," Eli sounded breathless. "Then if he shoots at you, at least you can defend yourself."

"No. If something goes wrong, you'll need it." He reached out and took hold of the doorknob. "Sorry about hitting you." He spoke to his brother with a nervous finality that made Caitlin's heart flutter. It was as if he wasn't expecting to come back and wanted to set things right.

She forced herself to look at Eli. His face was pale under the kitchen light; he looked tired—older all of a sudden. In spite of everything, she felt a pang of sympathy for him. Whatever he'd done to her, she didn't doubt how much he loved his brother.

"Forget it." He waved a hand in front of his face. "Just don't take any chances."

"Be careful." It was stupid really, but she couldn't think of what else to say apart from *don't get killed*.

Jace gave her a weak smile and opened the back door. A band of cool night air wafted into the stuffy kitchen. She wished she could slip outside, just for a moment and breathe in the clean air. Suddenly, staying barricaded in the house seemed worse than taking their chances with Blyte.

Jace turned side-on and slipped through the narrow opening. She thought of darting out after him, running down to the river. Going anywhere as long as she was out of the house and away from Eli. Before she could force her jittering legs to move, the door whispered closed and Jace was gone.

In the silence that followed, she strained to hear her brother-in-law's movements. Faint sounds, feet moving over the deck? Or maybe it was the blood pumping in her ears.

"He'll be okay," Eli broke the silence, speaking as if she'd asked a question. She wondered if he was reassuring her or himself.

Chapter Seven

Twin bars of artificial light tumbled from the high-set kitchen windows, hitting the deck in pearly lines. The shallow light was enough for Jace to make his way to the steps leading down to the grass. Beyond that, there was mostly blackness. He'd barely reached the edge of the platform before he realised his flip-flops had to go. *Why didn't I put my trainers on?* It seemed like such and obvious thing to do, he couldn't believe he hadn't thought of it before.

He kicked off the noisy rubber beach sandals and padded down the steps. The night air played over his arms and face, drying the sweat that clung to his skin like a soggy blanket. In the distance, he thought he caught a glimpse of the water, but with almost no moonlight, it was difficult to be sure.

He turned left and began following the faint outline of bushes towards the corner of the house. It had only been three weeks since he'd worked on building the deck, so the garden layout was still fresh in his mind. He knew the back of the house was flanked by bushy shrubs. Still he moved slowly, taking a few steps then stopping to listen.

Once he reached the corner, light from the sitting room windows spilled in narrow shafts, dotting the way forward. If Eli and Cat were doing their part, they'd be near the front door keeping Blyte occupied. He glanced back. The deck looked distant, little more than a silver smudge in the dark. If anything went wrong, would he have time to make it back? Even if he did reach the back door, he doubted Eli and Cat could move the fridge and let him in before Blyte was on top of him.

Micky Blyte wasn't living in the house when Jace worked on the deck, but the man had shown up a few times to check on the tradesmen. Jace only spoke to him once, but had the distinct impression he was hard-bitten, maybe ex-military. Physically, Blyte was only a little bigger than average. Jace definitely had a height and weight advantage, but Blyte had the look of someone who knew how to handle himself—something in his eyes and the way he carried himself. Jace didn't want a confrontation with the guy, not if he could help it.

He stepped around the corner of the house. It would be safer to stay out of the light, so Jace made the decision to go wide and skirt just beyond the rectangles of illumination. That way, he could still follow the line of the house but wouldn't risk being seen.

He moved right, crouched slightly and slipped amongst the trees. The sound of his bare feet on the dry leaves and twigs seemed deafening against the dull clicking and chirping of insects. He stepped forward, trying to come down on his toes, but it seemed however he moved, there was no escaping the noise. A few more steps and a needle of pain shot through his big toe.

He sucked in a breath through clenched teeth and stooped low. Cursing himself for not putting on shoes, he felt his injured toe. His fingers found something sharp, by the feel of it a small stick, wedged under his toenail. Grasping the stick, he took a breath and pulled. The pain flashed through his foot, white-hot in its intensity as a small shaft of dry wood tore through the soft flesh beneath his toenail.

He straightened and realised his fingers were slippery with blood. Grateful it was too dark to see the damage to his toe or the blood, he wiped his hand on the front of his t-shirt and moved forward. Ten metres or so and he'd be at the front of the house. He glanced up at one of the rectangular windows. Eli and Cat would be in position now, waiting to hear the double *beep* as he unlocked the car. He took another step and froze. Somewhere in the dark, a twig snapped.

Blyte had heard him and was somewhere nearby moving in on him. It was the only explanation. He considered running, breaking from the trees and barrelling toward the front of the house. His head whipped right. Had something rustled in the unseen branches? His breath came in pants, shallow and fast.

Another crackle, this time behind him. He had to make a decision: move or stay frozen and wait to be discovered. He could feel trails of sweat running down his neck and sides. Resisting the urge to bolt like a wild rabbit, he took a step forward, then another. It was only a few metres to the edge of the building. If he could make it that far, the car would be in sight.

Jace reached the front of the house. There had been no more rustling or movement from the trees or surrounding bush, but something was wrong. At this distance, he should have been able to hear Blyte talking to Eli. Jace ran his fingers over his face wiping the moisture away as he tried to think. Just because Blyte wasn't answering, didn't mean he wasn't there. Jace swapped the poker from one hand to the other and rubbed his sweaty palm on the leg of his shorts.

Like the side of the building, the windows at the front were set at least a head taller than Jace. He could see snatches of the gravel driveway and a few patches of grass, beyond that the outlines of both vehicles were little more than inky blurs. The smaller of the two shapes had to be Eli's car. Jace would have to make it past the other vehicle and then around the car to the driver's seat.

The safest path would be out and around the back of Blyte's vehicle. He'd be most vulnerable for the first five metres when he'd have to leave the cover of the bushes and dart across the grass. If he kept low and moved fast, there was little chance of being spotted.

Jace pulled the car keys out of his pocket and gripped the clicker, he wanted to be ready when he reached the driver's door. Poker in one hand, keys in the other, he bent his knees and shuffled out from the side of the house. The cold grass felt soothing on the soles of his feet. He edged out and slightly to the left, trying to get a look at the main entrance before he bolted.

The front door was a dark smudge flanked by brickwork. Jace craned his neck but couldn't make out a human shape near the entrance. He listened for voices but heard only the lone cry of an owl in the distant trees. Where were Eli and Cat? Surely they'd be calling to Blyte, trying to engage him with questions or demands.

Jace swore under his breath. Something was wrong. They wouldn't leave him hanging like this unless there was a problem. He could feel his pulse thumping in his ears. He thought of turning around and making his way back to the deck but then they'd be back where they started. Besides, he'd gotten the three of them into this mess in the first place. He thought of his brother. Jace had been so angry with him for what he was doing to Cat, it was tearing the brothers apart. Maybe if Jace stepped up for once and took responsibility, he could put things right. Then there was Cat. He couldn't bear to see her so frightened. If anything happened to her… He couldn't let himself go in that direction.

There was no more time to waste, he broke from the cover of the house and made for the cars. He'd made it less than a metre when something crashed through the trees. Jace pivoted and tried to turn but his left foot, slippery with blood, slid at an awkward angle and he lost his balance. At the same time as his knee hit the grass, a blow to his back knocked the air out of his lungs and sent him crashing to the ground writhing in pain. He tried to catch his breath, but his chest refused to heave. He heard grunting from above him. Something thick and coarse slipped down over his face and drew tight around his throat. Panicked and desperate for air, Jace pushed up in an attempt to stand but a crushing weight dropped onto his back mashing his face into the grass. He bucked and then lay still.

Chapter Eight

"We'd better get this against the door." Eli pressed his back to the fridge, knees bent. "Give me a hand?"

Caitlin joined him, her arm touching his. When they were both in place, Eli nodded for her to push. The hulking appliance tipped, almost toppling over then thumped down. "Get lower." Eli bent his knees. "Like this."

Both crouching like Sumo wrestlers, they used their legs and backs to force movement. Caitlin felt like her knees would give out under the strain as the fridge inched forward, casters tearing across the stone floor. She turned her head towards Eli. The tendons in his neck were straining against his skin as if they might push through. The appliance shuddered to a stop so suddenly, Caitlin's feet slid out from under her.

"You okay?" Eli offered her his hand. Her mind flashed back to the text message. *You look otherworldly.*

"I'm fine." She scrambled up ignoring his outstretched hand and brushing at her butt. "We should get to the front door, before Jace reaches the car."

Eli blocked her way. "Look, about what I said earlier... I didn't mean to—"

"You mean when you called me a slut?" She forced herself to meet his gaze.

"That was wrong of me, I know. I can't explain how it made me feel when I heard you talking to the doctor." His eyes glistened as if fighting back tears. "But I thought you were…" He hesitated as if at a loss, not sure how to finish.

"Perfect?" Caitlin spat out the word. It had taken all this time for her to realise what all this was about. Eli's need for perfection. Perfection in how he wanted his possessions to be arranged. Everything had to be just so, even his wife. On some level, she'd always known she could never measure up to his standards, that's why she'd eaten herself up trying to please him. But seeing the text message had changed everything. As much as his betrayal hurt, it also set her free.

"I'm sorry I hurt you." He looked down, defeated like a child who'd learned the tooth fairy's not real.

"We need to help Jace." There was so much more she wanted to say, but what good would it do? Their marriage was over. Each time she told herself, turned the words over in her mind, a little more weight fell from her shoulders.

"Yeah. Right." He rolled his shoulders and when he looked up, the tears were gone. Or maybe they'd never been there. Maybe he felt as relieved as her.

She followed him through to the sitting room, rubber-soled tennis shoes almost soundless on the stone floor. A quick glance towards the study confirmed the door was closed. She wondered if Felix was standing on the other side. The thought sent an icy shiver down her spine. What was it about the man that bothered her so much? The smell of him set her teeth on edge, but there was something else.

"We should get ready." Eli took up position behind the wooden cabinet and leaned towards the front door.

Before climbing up on the stool, Caitlin raced over to the coffee table and grabbed the candle holder. She pulled the half-melted candle free and tossed it on the table. The weight of the tarnished candlestick felt good in her hand, solid.

"Ready?" Eli whispered.

Caitlin nodded and took her place on the stool. The plan was pretty straightforward, when Jace unlocked the car, the beep would alert Blyte. At the same time, Caitlin and Eli would try and distract the man by turning the lights on and off and smashing a window. In the confusion, Jace would have the few seconds he needed to jump in the car and get going. At least that's how they hoped it would work. But first, they had to keep Blyte talking until Jace reached the car.

"Blyte?" Eli raised his voice. "Blyte?"

Caitlin pressed her hands to the glass and peered out. The night was impossibly dark, as if the house was no longer on the edge of the Myalup Forest but floating in deep space. She took a tremulous breath and forced herself to focus on the window. As her eyes adjusted to the dimness, she was able to see the outlines of the vehicles and bushes. Last time she'd looked out, Blyte's shoulder and arm were partially visible but now he was nowhere in sight.

"I can't see him," she kept her voice low, fighting the panic that threatened to swamp her.

"Blyte, are you out there? Blyte, I need to talk to you." Eli's voice was louder now, almost shouting. "Blyte?"

"He's not there."

Caitlin kept her face glued to the glass. "I can't see him anywhere. What do we do?"

"Shit." She heard her husband cursing and felt a flicker of anger.

"We need to *do* something. We can't just leave him out there." Caitlin dragged her gaze away from the window. They had to act quickly, there was no time for standing around.

The first thing she noticed was the look on Eli's face—fear mixed with shock. It was only then she noticed Felix. For a split second, she felt only confusion. Then the scene came together in stark detail. Felix had the gun in his hand and was pointing it at her husband.

"Get down." He spoke to her out of the side of his swollen mouth, keeping his eyes on Eli.

From where she stood on the stool, a circular bald spot on the top of Felix's head was clearly visible. For some reason, her eyes were drawn to the shiny pate and the way the light reflected making it seem like he had something oily on his scalp.

"Don't make me ask again." His voice, harsh and cold got her moving.

Caitlin made her way off the stool and onto the floor still clutching the candlestick. Her mind tried to make sense of what was happening. A few hours ago, they'd been having a barbeque and now they were prisoners in an isolated house with a guy holding a gun at them.

"Put that down and come over here." Felix jerked his chin towards Caitlin. It took her a second to process what he was telling her. She looked at the candlestick in her hand and realised he saw it as a potential weapon. She almost laughed but managed to clamp her mouth shut before the sound broke free.

Caitlin placed the candlestick on the stool and walked over to her husband. Her legs felt numb, as if she'd been sitting on them. For one horrifying second, she thought they'd collapse under her and she'd hit the floor. What then? Would he shoot her? The questions turned over in her head, one for each step she took. Eli's face floated ahead of her, pale and strained as he watched her progress.

The last time she remembered seeing the gun was in the kitchen. Eli put it on the island bench while they were talking. He must have left it there when they came through to the sitting room. Had Felix been waiting for a chance to get his hands on the weapon?

She stood beside her husband, her shoulder touching his arm just as it had only minutes ago when they were moving the fridge. Something touched her fingers. She almost gasped, but realised Eli was holding her hand. His breathing seemed too loud, she wanted to tell him to take deep breaths but all she could focus on was the black circle pointed towards them. The barrel of the gun trained on her like a dark empty eye.

"Don't do anything crazy," Eli's voice sounded hollow as if he spoke into the wind. "We're the ones trying to help you."

Felix's puffy face, one eye obscured by swelling, stretched into a lop-sided grin. One of his front teeth had been broken leaving a jagged line of white, stark against the dried blood on his lips. "By driving off and leaving me here."

"We were going to get help." Eli's hand felt slippery with sweat. "Look, you have to understand. We have no idea what's going on here, we just wanted to get help." Caitlin squeezed his fingers willing him to stop talking. Nothing he could say would make the man understand their reasoning. He was enjoying watching them squirm.

"Good idea. Only I'll go and you can wait here." The smile on Felix's face slipped away turning his features into a mask of bruised indifference.

When the gun fired, Caitlin heard an explosion of sound as if it came from inside her head and thumped the back of her ear drums. The roar seemed to go on and on, bouncing off the walls and blocking out every other noise. A blast of warm air hit her in the chest like a tepid snowball.

She blinked in flashes of colour and faces. It wasn't until the ringing blast faded that she realised she was screaming and there was blood streaming down her arm.

Chapter Nine

Jace stopped struggling. The sour taste of damp grass filled his mouth as the rope tightened around his neck. The weight on his back increased until he thought his shoulders would break under the load. With each breath, his lungs shuddered.

"I'm going to let you turn over, but if you try to run, you'll choke yourself." The voice was familiar, deep and gruff. "Nod if you understand."

Jace moved his chin, as close as he could come to nodding with his face mashed into the ground.

"Okay. When I say move, you turn." The rope tightened, bunching the skin against Jace's Adam's apple. "If you hear me, you better start nodding."

The increased pressure made it almost impossible to move, but Jace pulled in a breath and managed to jerk his head. The movement must have been enough because almost immediately the rope loosened a fraction allowing him room to swallow. The weight on his back shifted and then eased.

"Okay. Turn."

Jace did as the voice ordered and flopped over onto his back. Without the grass clogging his mouth, he was free to breathe in the night air. As his lungs filled, he tried to blink away the tears that filled his eyes. Stars wavered and then came into focus.

To his right, a narrow pool of bluish white light. He shifted his elbows trying to raise his head. "Slowly." The voice, definitely Blyte's, came from the same direction as the light.

With the rope still looped around his neck, it was impossible for Jace to move any other way but slowly. Pushing his forearms flat against the ground, he lifted his upper body into a sitting position. As his head came up, the pressure on the noose increased.

"Now." Blyte spoke from behind the light obscuring his face and body. "Tell me what the hell you're doing in my house."

Two lengths of striped rope, possibly used for abseiling, ran from the noose. One trailed over his shoulder and ran towards the trees, the other ran into the light. Judging by the tautness and the direction of Blyte's voice, Jace guessed the man held the end of the second line, pulling it tight or letting it loose when he wanted Jace to move.

Jace ran his fingers around the noose, pulling it forward slightly. As he did so, the pressure increased. "Stop fucking about and answer the question."

"I—" Jace's throat contracted. He hacked out a coughing breath and tried again. "I worked on your deck... With Lowman's Construction." The back of his throat burned as if he'd swallowed gravel. "I copied the key and brought my brother and his wife here for the weekend." In the darkness, he could feel his face burn with shame. He'd never stolen anything in his life, but now the words were out, he felt like a petty criminal. "I told them you were a mate of mine. None of this is their fault."

Jace waited, the hiss of insects sounded louder as if they were crowding in. "What's your name?"

"Jace. Jace Frost." He stared into the light but could only make out a dark form.

"Well, Jace, it doesn't matter whose fault this is. You and your family have wandered into a shit storm. The question is, what are we going to do about it?"

Jace's mind tried to fathom what Blyte was asking. If the man wanted him dead, he could have killed him by now. Maybe he could talk his way out of the mess he'd gotten everyone into; it was worth a chance.

"Look, we don't care what's going on here. Just let us leave and we won't say anything." He reached for something convincing. "I've broken the law by using your house. I'd be dropping myself in it if I went to the cops." His voice rasped as if he had a handful of dirt in his throat.

"I'd like to believe that, Jace. I really would, but I've worked on this too long and hard to have it fall apart now."

Jace felt his stomach clench. What did Blyte mean? Surely he wouldn't kill the three of them in cold blood. He searched for something to say that might convince the man to let them go, but his mind raced and all he could see was Felix's bruised and battered face. He'd seen what Blyte was capable of, would murder be a stretch for a man like him?

"Please, my brother and his wife have done nothing wrong. Don't hurt them, I'm begging you." Jace stared into the light, arms out, palms up.

"What do you think I am?" Blyte no longer sounded calm. "I'm not a murderer."

Jace felt a rush of relief. "Thank you. I promise we won't tell anyone what you're doing here."

"I can't let you leave."

"What? But you just said—"

"I'm not a murderer, but you and your family can't leave, *not yet*. I don't want to have to hurt you, but if you try to get away…" Blyte let out a tired breath. "I'll take whatever measure I feel necessary to stop you."

Jace shook his head. The rope burned into his skin making it difficult for him to focus and think clearly. He tried swallowing, the soft flesh in the back of his throat felt scarred and dry. He needed water, something to sooth the burning. He tried to ignore the pain and concentrate on what the man was saying. Something about not letting them go, yet.

"You said not yet… and earlier, you mentioned someone named Amy." He saw Blyte's shape move behind the light. He had his attention, maybe he was on to something. "Is this about a woman? Is that why you locked Felix in the cellar, because of a woman?"

Blyte's voice, when he answered was quieter. "She wasn't a woman. She was my thirteen-year-old sister." He hesitated. "Felix Holly abducted and murdered her fifteen years ago."

The words hit Jace like a physical blow. If what Blyte said was true, Eli and Cat were locked in the house with a killer. *No*, he corrected himself. A child killer.

"I'm sorry." It sounded lame but Jace didn't know what else to say. "If he did that, what you said–"

"Murdered my little sister?" Blyte's voice cracked. "He did, only the cops could never prove anything."

"So you brought him here to kill him?" Jace shifted his butt, moving a few centimetres closer to Blyte. In doing so, the rope slackened giving him a little more breathing room.

"I told you, I'm not a killer… I just want to know where she is so we can give her a proper burial. My mother's dying." Jace could hear the emotion in the man's voice. The light moved, Jace heard rustling. A lighter flared and for a second, he got a glimpse of Blyte's face, prominent jaw, and deep-set eyes. He lit a cigarette and then extinguished the flame. "She's got a couple of months at best. I want her to be able to bury her daughter before…" His words trailed off.

"So you were *beating* the answers out of him?" Jace finished for him. "Is that it?"

"Yep." The tip of the cigarette glowed red in the blackness.

Jace watched the light glowing, moving occasionally from Blyte's mouth to his hand. Felix's story was very different to Blyte's, yet Jace had no doubt Micky Blyte was telling the truth. Or what he believed to be the truth.

Jace opened his mouth to ask, *what now?* A thunderous crack pierced the night, silencing the clatter of insects and sending sleeping birds screeching from the surrounding trees. It took him a few seconds to understand what was happening. A gunshot, fired inside the house.

Chapter Ten

Fingers still wrapped around Caitlin's hand, Eli's weight sank pulling her down with him. He met the floor with a muffled thump. Then came a crack as his head hit stone. Caitlin sprawled over her husband, sounds were coming out of her mouth but she had no awareness of what she was saying. There was so much blood and the smell mingled with spent gunpowder filled her nose.

"Caitlin. It's—I'm–" Eli's eyes rolled in her direction, shiny with panic and shock.

The wound was on his side, just below his ribs—a mushy hole bubbling with dark blood. Caitlin, now on her knees beside him, felt his blood pooling around her calves. She held her hands above the wound, wanting to stop the bleeding but afraid to touch him.

"It's okay. Lie still. It's okay." She pressed her fingers to his face. "Don't move. It's okay." The words were meaningless but Eli responded to her voice, his eyes fixed on her and he nodded.

"I can't… It… I'm cold." His words were slurred and fading.

Caitlin looked around searching for help but knowing none would come. Felix stood to Eli's right, gun in hand.

"You shot him!" She screamed the words as if he didn't know what he'd done. "He's… hurt." *Dying* was what she wanted to say, but the terrified look in her husband's eyes stopped her.

Felix shrugged. His gaze hovered on Eli for a few seconds as if puzzled by what was happening to him. When he finally looked at her, Caitlin couldn't believe what she saw. Even with the bruises and swelling, there was no mistaking the indifference on the man's face. He watched Eli as if he were nothing more than a fly buzzing on the window sill.

"Get up." He waved the gun in Eli's direction. "Do it or the next one goes in his head."

Caitlin shook her head. "Didn't you hear me? He needs help. We've got–"

"Get. Up." Felix's voice remained calm. He pointed the gun at Eli's head.

"Okay. Okay." Caitlin touched her husband's shoulder. His skin felt devoid of warmth as if he'd been bathed in ice. She stumbled to her feet, almost slipping on the blood pooling around her.

Felix fixed his gaze on her. "Take off your dress."

The words filled her head, but didn't compute. "What?" She knew what he'd said but couldn't understand his meaning.

"Take off your dress." His face was emotionless, one brown eye regarded her.

Caitlin looked down at her husband. His eyes were wide, blinking rapidly. Could he hear what was happening? In spite of everything that had happened between them, she hoped not. If these were his last moments, better they be empty than filled with horror.

"I—I don't understand." She stuttered out the words, playing for time.

"I think you do." Felix moved the gun between her and Eli. "I don't want to shoot you." He pointed the gun at her husband. "But him." He shrugged. "I don't mind."

"All right." Caitlin held her hands up palms facing him. "Okay, but not here. Not in front of my husband." Her voice shook. "Please."

Felix's eyes flicked from her to the door. He seemed to be thinking. It had been only moments since Eli was shot, but Caitlin's mind started working again. She forced herself to focus, not on the blood but on how she was going to get the two of them out—alive.

"You want some privacy?" Felix gave a half grin that made Caitlin's stomach lurch. "Let's go back to where all this started." He held out his arm gesturing towards the kitchen. There were bruises, dark purple like an over-ripe plum dotted on his upper arm. "Why don't you lead the way?"

He meant to take her to the cellar. The wall, spattered with blood flashed in her mind. If she let him get her in that room… An image formed in her mind. The mouth of a cave… Her thoughts faltered. She wouldn't go in there, he'd have to kill her first. "Okay."

She took a step and something caught her ankle. "No… No, don't." Eli's fingers clamped around her leg, shaking as if he were having a seizure. His eyes pleading with her. "Caitlin. No."

"Huh." Felix frowned down at Eli. "From what I heard, you didn't have much regard for your wife. It's a bit late to play the hero now, don't you think?"

Eli's mouth opened but nothing came out. He raised his right arm and tried to grab Felix's torn trouser leg, but Felix was too quick. He stepped back and shot out a bare foot, kicking Eli in the shoulder.

"No." Caitlin reached out to Felix, but was too late to stop another kick from landing. This time in Eli's side.

Eli's body rocked slightly and his grip on her ankle released. He groaned, a weak sound, little more than a deep breath. Caitlin's vision blurred with tears.

"Let's get going." Felix spoke in a cheerful upbeat way as if they were late for a dinner date.

Caitlin stumbled towards the kitchen, tennis shoes squeaking with blood as they slid over the stone floor. She didn't dare look over her shoulder. Not because of Felix, but so she wouldn't have to see her husband's pleading eyes follow her progress.

When they reached the kitchen, Felix stepped around her and stood beside the cellar door. The lights were still on, she could see the same wedge of stairs that had so intrigued her when they first opened the door. Now they only made her shudder.

"You're older than I usually like." He held the gun down at his side. "Pretty but older." He sighed. "But beggars can't be choosers." He laughed, a porcine noise that made her want to clutch her head and scream. "After you." He jerked his chin, motioning for her to go ahead of him down the stairs. "You should be thanking me, he wasn't much of a husband. A bit of a weak character really, he would have turned me over to Blyte to save his sad skin."

She forced her feet to move, legs wet with Eli's blood. When she reached the doorway, Felix turned slightly half blocking the entrance. He wasn't a big man, no taller than about 5' 8", and wiry, yet somehow he managed to fill the space giving her no choice but to slide between his chest and the frame.

Up close, the smell of him was inescapable, thick and earthy. Caitlin held her breath and turned so her back was to him as she slipped through the opening. Closing her eyes, she wedged her body towards the stairs. For the briefest of moments, his breath touched her shoulders, hot and damp. In spite of her best efforts, she let go of the breath and gasped. Felix snorted out another laugh and made a wet kissing noise as she pulled away and scrambled onto the stairs.

When they first found him in the hidden room, he seemed badly injured. She remembered the way he clutched his side begging them for help, letting Jace half carry him to the study. Had it all been an act? The bruises and the dirt were real, those he couldn't fake, but the rest of the story had to be lies. Blyte warned them, but they hadn't listened.

"That's it." Felix spoke over her shoulder. "Keep going."

Caitlin descended the steps, knees locking, resisting each bend. Halfway down, something touched her shoulder making her jump and almost lose her balance. She turned her head coming face to face with the barrel of the gun. Felix chuckled and pushed the gun into her shoulder. "Get moving, we've lots to do."

She didn't want to ponder the meaning behind his words. If she didn't think of a way out soon, they'd be in the secret room, with the smell and the blood. The saliva in her mouth evaporated making it difficult for her to swallow. The panicky desire to escape at all cost snatched her breath away. She tried to control her breathing and think. With each stride, she heard the sound of the gun firing and saw the blood gushing out of Eli's shredded flesh.

They were almost at the bottom of the stairs. Her focus narrowed to the concrete floor, her black tennis shoes. She had to act, do something—stop it happening to her again. She wasn't a frightened little girl anymore. *I'd rather die than go back.*

She rounded the foot of the stairs, heart pounding at a sickening rate. The sour smell of spilled wine filled her mouth and nose. Shards of smashed wine bottle littered the floor turning the area between the stairs and hidden room into a mine field. With the gun pointed at her back, Caitlin knew her chances of escaping were almost nil. Now less than eight metres between her and the room, she took her chance.

Falling on already quivering legs wasn't a challenge. She let her knees fold and hit the concrete. A splinter of glass pierced her calf making her cry out, adding believability to the fall. Behind her, Felix cursed and landed a bare-footed kick on her rear end. The blow hard enough to send her sprawling forward to where a hunk of thick green glass glittered under the light.

Caitlin's palms slapped the floor, coming down on a carpet of tiny shards. She lurched right and snatched the large piece of jagged glass, praying Felix's view of her hands was blocked by her head and back.

"You really are losing appeal." There was irritation in his voice but no sign of alarm.

She pulled her hand back, holding the glass close to her chest. He was expecting her to stand. Instead, she pulled herself onto one knee drawing out the moment by swaying off balance.

"Get on your fucking feet." The mocking playfulness vanished, replaced by vicious anger.

Caitlin's heart jittered, missed a beat. If she failed, he'd kill her. *He'll kill me anyway—when he's done.* His hand snaked under her left arm and clamped her flesh like a vice. Yanking, he pulled her to her feet. She let herself be positioned, limp like a doll filled with sawdust. He dragged her along.

His chest only centimetres from her back, Caitlin swung around and faced him. Taken by surprise, Felix stared into her face, not noticing her hand. She brought the glass up and jammed the jagged shaft into his left shoulder.

He shrieked, mouth open and nose wrinkled with pain. Caitlin held onto the glass, twisting and pushing it into his flesh. Her hand stung as if too close to a flame. Felix let go of her other arm and stumbled back a few steps.

She let go of the piece of broken bottle and for a second stood frozen, staring at what she'd done. The glass buried in his shoulder protruded like a hideous transparent tentacle.

"You bitch," spittle flew from his mouth. He reached for her and screamed as the shard sticking out of his flesh moved up and down.

Caitlin drew her knee up and stamped on his bare foot, turning her heel back and forth as if stubbing out a cigarette. The gun hit the floor with a heavy *clunk*. Felix tried to raise his injured foot, but stumbled to his left. It was the best chance she'd get. Caitlin shoved him and ran for the stairs.

Not daring to waste precious seconds looking back, she took the steps two at a time. At the top, she skidded into the kitchen pulling the door closed behind her with a *thwack* that rattled the hinges. There was no lock. For a second, she held the knob, eyes dancing over the room in search of any way of securing the door. Almost instantly, she spotted the long black extension cord Jace and Eli had pulled from the fridge.

Hands shaking, she darted for the cord. Snatching it up and sliding back to the door just as the sound of feet thumping the stairs came below. With time running out, she wound the cord around the knob. Barely noticing the blood on her hands, Caitlin raced to the fridge. Wedged against the back door, the twin handles faced front. She tied the black cord around the handle on the left, securing the knot just as the cellar door rattled.

The knob turned. With a jerk, the door pulled inwards then stopped. Caitlin pressed her back against the fridge, palms flat on the cold metal. Her heart rate slowed slightly, but still beat at an unnatural pace.

"What the hell," Felix's voice came from the five-centimetre gap between the door and the frame. To Caitlin's relief, the cord held allowing the door to only open a fraction.

His fingers curled through the gap, searching for the obstruction. The grubby appendages reminded Caitlin of earth worms squirming in the soil. She eased herself away from the fridge trying to move as silently as possible. The door shuddered then slammed shut. She froze half-way between the fridge and the island bench almost directly ahead of the door.

Long strands of damp hair clung to her face. She pressed her lips together and stared at the door, trying to guess what he might be doing on the other side. The cellar door opened with a jolt, violent and sudden. Caitlin pressed her hands to the sides of her face and watched as if hypnotised. The door opened and slammed over and over like it was caught in cyclonic winds.

With each yank, the black extension cord twanged. It wouldn't hold forever. She had to move. As if sensing her thoughts, the slamming stopped. The door hung open a fraction revealing nothing but pale light.

"Please?" Felix's swollen lips appeared in the gap. "I'm sorry. I wasn't going to do anything." Two fingers curled around the door. "I know I scared you, but I panicked. You've got to believe me."

The change in his voice, from fury to pleading was almost as frightening as the sight of his fleshy mouth in the gap of the door. A disconnect between her brain and legs made it difficult for her to move.

"I didn't want to hurt anyone, but you were going to leave me here." He sniffed. "I'll give you the gun, please just let me out." If she hadn't seen what he did to Eli with her own eyes, she would have thought his regret sincere, pathetic almost. "You hurt me, it's bad. I'm bleeding... I just want to go home. I'm so sorry."

She let her hands drop from her face. Nothing he said could block the memory of his half-smile and snorting laugh. *You're older than I usually like.*

"You're a liar," her voice shook so violently, she barely recognised it as her own. "I know what you are, I've met your sort before." She should have been running, trying to help her husband, but something uncurled in the pit of her stomach. Something small and clenched, wrapped in years of secrets, shame, and anger. "You're an animal. We should have *let* Blyte torture you." She could feel tears running down her cheeks, wet globs plopping onto her chest.

"Open the door," His voice dropped to a stage whisper. "What did that big dumb brother-in-law of yours call you?" He giggled, the sound reminded her of a hungry pig. "Oh, I remember, Cat. Come here Kitty Cat. Come and let me out."

She spun away and sprinted out of the kitchen just as the cellar door started banging again.

Eli lay where he fell, near the front door. Caitlin belted across the room, skidding to a halt a few metres from her husband's unmoving body. His arms were at his sides. *What if he's dead?* The rush of adrenalin that gave her enough strength to escape Felix ebbed, leaving her limbs trembling.

She approached him slowly, terrified of touching him but desperate to help. A coppery sweet smell surrounded him as did a pool of blood. Her gut clenched and bile rose in her throat.

"Eli?" the word came out around a breathy whisper.

His skin was the colour of wet paper. She knelt and touched his face, startled by the lack of warmth. "Eli, wake up," her voice broke. "Please, Eli?"

His eyes opened and rolled towards her. Caitlin pressed her hand to his cheek, her hair brushing his skin. Tears blurred her vision turning his face into a bleary mask. "I'm going to get something to cover you."

"Where… did?" His eyelids fluttered and then flew open. "Did he…"

She let go of his face long enough to swipe the tears away. "No. No, I'm fine. I locked him in the cellar. Eli grimaced and let out a groan. She wasn't sure if he was responding to her words or fighting the pain. "I'll be back, okay?"

She started to stand but he stopped her. His hand on her arm cold and clammy. "Can he get out?"

The sound of the cellar door slamming continued from the kitchen. She had no doubt Felix would work his way out. What she didn't know was how long she had before he came looking for her.

"No, I don't think so," she lied. "I'll be back."

Caitlin raced to the study and snatched up the yellow blanket they'd used to cover Felix. She caught a whiff of something rotten and dirty. The smell might have been her imagination, she wasn't sure. But if there were anything else, she would have flung the rug aside. Unless she took the time to go upstairs, it was all she had so she tucked it under her arm.

Eli was losing blood—fast. She needed something to press on the wound and slow down the loss. The study was little more than a bare room, dressed carefully but without the things people usually dot around their home. Now that she thought about it, the whole house was just like the study. At first glance, a holiday home, but really a carefully staged façade. The real heart of this home was the cellar, everything else was part of the disguise. The realisation sent a chill down her spine.

With the rug under her arm, she returned to her husband. In the background, the sound of Felix opening and closing the door continued—every bang bringing closer the moment when the evil creature in the cellar would be set free. She wished she could cover her ears and block out the dreadful pounding.

Caitlin covered her husband with the yellow blanket taking care to tuck it around his feet. She pulled the rug up to his chin, but couldn't help noticing the circle of blood already soaking through the woollen fabric. He was losing too much blood, and judging by the way he was shivering, going into shock. If she didn't get him help soon, he'd die. The very least she could do to slow things down, was find something to press on his wound.

"Eli." At the sound of his name, his lids fluttered, but didn't open. "I'm going to the kitchen, I'll be right back." She wanted to say more. "Hang on, please."

He made no response.

The kitchen was the last place in the house Caitlin wanted to be. She entered as silently as possible hoping Felix wouldn't hear her approach. No sooner had she reached the bench than the banging ceased. The door stood ajar. Caitlin held her breath. The two tea towels she and Jace had fooled around with that afternoon were folded and stacked on the bench top beside the oven.

"Is that you, Kitty Cat?" The voice hissed out of the gap in the cellar door.

"Shut up." She should have ignored him, but the sound of his voice gnawed at her jangling nerves.

She edged her way to the stove making sure she kept clear of the cellar door and the extension cord. Out of the corner of her eye, she noticed the bloody handprints she'd left on the doors of the fridge. The blood looked almost unreal, so bright and stark against the white. Without thinking, she rubbed her hands on her dress.

"If you let Blyte in, he'll kill you." She could hear Felix panting now, as if exhausted. "Let me out and I'll help you."

Caitlin grabbed the tea towels and left the room.

Kneeling next to Eli, she folded the fabric into two ten-centimetre squares. The blood on the blanket hadn't spread much since she went to the kitchen. Good or bad sign, she wasn't sure.

Steeling herself, Caitlin pulled the blanket away from the wound. A breath caught in her throat. The area around the entry point looked shredded and puckered, the underlying tissue, bloody and raw. Bile, that she'd forced back only moments before threatened to rise again. Only by taking slow, even breaths and forcing her mind to latch on to what had to be done, was she able to continue.

She held the folded square to the wound. *Apply pressure.* They were about the only two words she remembered from a long-ago first aid class in high school. She pressed on the fabric trying to ignore the squelch that come from the pulpy mess under the tea towel. Eli groaned and opened his eyes.

"I'm sorry." She hoped she wasn't doing more harm than good.

"Where…is he?" Eli's lips, tinged with violet, moved slowly as if the effort of speaking drained whatever strength he had left.

"Don't worry about him." She couldn't resist snatching a glance towards the kitchen.

The constant slamming ceased. The silence was worse. At least when Felix was banging the door, she knew what he was up to. The thought of his mouth in the crack of the door, whispering and cajoling made the hairs on the back of her neck stand on end. How long would it be before he managed to break through the door or loosen the extension cord?

Eli's eyes were closed again, his breathing slow and shallow, the tea towel, slippery and sodden beneath her fingers. Rather than removing the bloody wad, she pressed the second tea towel over the top and continued to keep the pressure on the wound. Around her, the house fell silent.

Her eyes lingered on the fringed edge of the blanket, once a cheerful yellow, now crimson and sitting in a pool of rapidly congealing blood. She tried to recall a time when she'd felt this lonely. Her memory responded by spitting up an image of sunlight, dappled through the window of a moving car. Voices, like a forgotten echo, raised in cheerful song. The bloody mess on the floor distorted and she let out a sob that quickly turned into a wail.

"Is someone there?" The voice came from the front door and was quickly followed by a rapid succession of knocks.

Caitlin stifled a scream and let go of the wadded-up tea towel. Since Felix appeared with the gun, there'd been no time to worry about Blyte. Now he was at the door, Caitlin realised she'd heard nothing from her brother-in-law since he left the house.

Over the last half an hour, the world had turned upside-down leaving Caitlin so off balance, she felt like she was standing on the roof of a skyscraper. Trying to decide what to do next made her feel like she tottered towards the edge about to fall. Thoughts and doubts tugged her in different directions until she was paralysed.

"I heard the gun," Blyte's voice was deep, almost commanding. "Has someone been shot?"

Caitlin wanted to answer—ask for help. But could she take the risk not knowing if the man on the other side of the door was as dangerous as the one in the cellar? Hands balled into fists, she grappled with the possibilities. This strange house of horrors belonged to Blyte, what did that say about the man? What about Jace? He'd gone outside to face Blyte and vanished.

"Can you hear me, Felix?" The name alone sent a shudder of panic through Caitlin's body. She listened as Blyte continued. "What have you done to those people?" Blyte's voice rose to a threatening growl, "You sick little freak, let me in."

Caitlin winced. The very air seemed charged with violence as if the house itself fed the stuff into its occupants like poison gas. Now she was its prisoner and whichever way she turned it offered only more terror.

"You won't get away with it, not this time." Blyte thumped the door, sending a shudder through the heavy wood. "I won't let you. You got off easy last time, a few years in the hospital dribbling lies about how fucked up your parents made you and all the time laughing about how smart you think you are." There wasn't just anger in the man's voice, but pain. "You can't stay in there forever." Another thump. "Tell me what you did with my sister!" Blyte's voice broke. The hopeless desolation in his plea made her heart ache.

Amy. Suddenly everything made sense. Felix *was* dangerous. No, more than dangerous, insane—a predator. Earlier on Blyte said all he wanted was answers. She realised he didn't bring Felix to the house because Blyte enjoyed torturing people. He'd locked Felix in the cellar out of desperation. He wanted to know what happened to his sister, Amy. With understanding came a flicker of hope. *Maybe Blyte isn't the enemy.* He might be her only hope.

"Where's my brother-in-law?" If she was going to trust him, she had to know what he'd done with Jace.

"Who's there? I heard a shot, what happened?"

"Answer my question. Where's my brother-in-law?" Caitlin hoped her voice sounded stronger than she felt.

"He's fine. Tried to get to the car, so I tied him up round the side of the house." Blyte sounded irritated at having to explain himself. "Now tell me what's going on in there. Better still, open the door."

Caitlin had no way of knowing if he was telling the truth. For all she knew, Jace was lying face down out in the dark somewhere. But time was running out, if Eli didn't get medical help soon, he'd die. She had no choice but to take a chance on Micky Blyte.

"My husband's been shot." Her voice echoed off the walls. "He's badly hurt, unconscious. Felix tried to…" She couldn't bring herself to put it into words. "He's got the gun."

"Jesus." The word whistled out in a rush of either anger or surprise, she wasn't sure which. "Where is he?"

"I locked him in the cellar, but the way I rigged the door won't hold long."

His next question took her by surprise. "What's your name?"

She looked down at her blood-stained hands, still clenched into fists. "Caitlin." She could feel tears welling up in her eyes, turning the horrific scene into a hazy red blur. "I'm Caitlin Frost."

"I'm Micky." The exchange of names seemed formal, almost old-fashioned under the circumstances. The urge to laugh bubbled up Caitlin's throat. Instead she gritted her teeth, afraid the laughter would get tangled in her mouth and come out as a pitiful shriek.

"Caitlin, open the door." Something in his voice, a solidness that reminded her of old cowboy movies she'd watched with Eli. Whatever it was, made her want to trust him.

"Okay, it's barricaded with a big wooden cabinet. I don't know if I can move it."

For a second there was silence, the only sounds came from Eli's shallow breathing and her pulse beating in her ears. The moment stretched. She wondered if he'd simply walked away and left her. The thought took root and she felt panic turning in her stomach like a spinning top with sharp edges.

"Unlock the door first." When he spoke, Caitlin felt a rush of relief. An hour ago she'd been terrified of Blyte. She'd imagined him as a giant with burning red eyes ready to tear them all limb from limb. Now, she'd pinned all her hopes on a man she'd never even seen. Yet, rather than seeming to be taking a huge risk, her gut told her she could trust Blyte. More than trust him. Something in his voice, pulled at her soul as if he knew her pain. An impossible rush of emotion that made no sense, but in the midst of the nightmare, she was ready to follow her instincts. "See if you can shift it. I only need enough room to get my shoulder through and then I can push from my side."

"Okay. Yes, I'll try." Before standing, she pulled the blanket back up and tucked it around Eli's shoulders.

Legs numb from kneeling, Caitlin moved to the door. She scooted around the cabinet to the right and slid the heavy bolt back from across the top of the door. The bolt moved with a dusty metal-on-metal grind. Once more, the slab reminded her of a church door.

"Okay," she raised her voice so Blyte could hear her. "Bolt's undone. I'm going to try to shift the cabinet." It felt good to be doing something, making progress instead of giving in to fear.

The cabinet looked like it weighed at least a hundred kilos, the far side wedged flat against the door. Caitlin tried standing in front of the heavy piece of furniture and pulling but quickly gave up on the idea.

"How's it going?"

"I'm trying to get a…" She stopped. Her attention had been so focused on talking to Micky and getting the door open, she hadn't realised how silent the house had become until the hush was broken.

A twanging, barely audible, like the noise a skipping rope makes when pulled taunt. Caitlin tilted her head to the side and brushed back her hair, straining to hear.

"What's happening?" Standing next to the door, Micky's voice sounded so close, so solid.

Caitlin opened her mouth to answer when she heard another twang from the kitchen. A warm trickle of sweat ran down her chest.

She pressed her face to the edge of the door and whispered, "I think he's coming."

Chapter Eleven

Jace worked the noose, pressing and pushing the skin on his neck with one hand and then shifting the rope a centimetre at a time with the other. Progress was slow and painful. With each shift of the rope, his skin caught and snagged against the noose. In minutes, his face was covered in a mask of sweat and his throat burned with thirst.

When Blyte left, he took the light with him, leaving Jace in almost pitch darkness. He could hear a voice from the front of the house. Blyte was talking to someone, but Jace could only hear one side of the conversation and that was muffled at best. The only thing he was sure of was the shot. Someone had fired the gun.

With his fingers pressed to his throat, he could feel his pulse racing just under the skin. His imagination threw up a tangle of possibilities about what was happening inside the house, none of them pleasant. He pulled in a breath through his nose and gave the rope a final twist bringing it to a stop against his Adam's apple.

From what he could tell, Blyte had rigged some sort of two-rope binding running between a couple of trees. Jace cursed as he fumbled over the complicated knot that held the noose in place. *Where did this guy learn how to tie knots?* At this rate, he'd still be trying to figure his way out of the noose when the sun came up.

Jace slumped from his knees back onto his butt. The sound of frogs croaking out their night-time song surrounded him, growing louder by the minute. His mind went back to the gunshot.

Could it have been an accident? Maybe Eli dropped the gun and it went off. It was plausible. Eli had never really handled a gun. Outside of a few hunting trips with their uncle when they were teenagers, neither he nor his brother had fired a gun.

No, he corrected himself. *I don't know what Eli does, not anymore.* It was true, he'd only found out about his brother's affair by accident. Running into him in the city three weeks ago, Jace remembered the look in his brother's eyes. A shifting nervousness belonging to someone with a secret. If not for that look, Jace might have believed his brother's story about having lunch with a client, despite the way the fresh-faced brunette in the red dress held Eli's hand, clutching it close to her slim body as they stepped onto the street.

Jace ran into them coming out of a boutique hotel on Adelaide Terrace and almost kept walking. At first glance, he barely recognised the smiling man with the hot little brunette as his brother. Jace snatched a second look at the couple. Maybe because they looked so blissful, or maybe the angle of the man's shoulders, the familiar tilt of the head, was what drew Jace's stare.

"Eli?" Jace had spoken his brother's name and watched the smile slide away, replaced by a look stricken with shame.

"Hi." The smile came back on Eli's face, but gone was the carefree beam. Replaced by a frozen mask of false pleasantness. "This is Sherri. She's a rep for Ulton Pharmaceuticals." Eli slipped his hand free of Sherri's grasp, ignoring the questioning look on the woman's face.

"Right." Jace, wearing sawdust-covered khakis, nodded to the woman at his brother's side.

"This is my brother, Jace." Eli spoke rapidly, not giving Sherri a chance to respond.

For a moment, the three of them had stood on the terrace as office workers swarmed past, side-stepping the group who dared hold up the flow. Jace knew his brother was waiting for him to speak, to break the tension. Maybe even buy into the little charade. Instead he focused on Eli's eyes. They skipped from the line of traffic rolling past to the entrance to the hotel, anywhere but Jace's face.

Finally, it was the woman who broke the spell. "Well, I'd better get going. More meetings this afternoon." She nodded to Jace and flashed a dazzling smile. "It was nice to meet you."

Jace nodded but kept his mouth clamped shut, knowing if he spoke, he'd say too much. He knew Eli and Caitlin were having problems. He'd been with his brother at the hospital when he overheard his wife telling the doctor about an abortion she'd had at fifteen. Eli's reaction had been beyond all reason. He'd stormed out of the hospital as if he'd just found out Caitlin had shot the Pope. But now this. An affair. None of it had made sense.

"Yeah. I'll walk you to your car." Eli looked relieved to have an excuse to end the awkward meeting. "Nice seeing you. I'll call you later." He didn't wait for Jace to respond, but stepped around his brother and headed towards the corner.

Jace turned and watched them walk away. Eli took long purposeful strides, his arms stiff at his side like a man who knew he was being watched. Sherri tottered along behind him, almost stumbling on a set of heels meant more for a nightclub than a business meeting.

Eli's promised call never came. That was when the idea of spending a weekend in Blyte's empty holiday house really took hold. He'd told himself he wanted to help Eli and Cat put their marriage back together, but it wasn't true. The real reason he wanted them at the house was darker, selfish. *I wanted her to see what a shit he is.* Jace shifted his butt, feeling the damp ground seeping through the fabric of his shorts. He wanted Cat. He'd always wanted her and he despised his brother for being too weak to appreciate what he had. Jace knew he'd messed everything up. Whatever happened, whoever got hurt, the blame would be on his head.

He gave the knot another tug. His hands dropped to his thighs. It was no use, Blyte's knots were too complicated. At this angle, in the dark, he'd never get them undone. Worse than being trapped in the middle of nowhere was the realisation he'd let Cat down. If she were hurt in any way, how would he live with himself?

Jace curled his hand into a fist and hammered it down on his leg sending a buzz of agony through his thigh. Something solid jarred against his knuckles. He opened his mouth ready to let loose with a stream of invective and stopped. With the speed of a light bulb firing to life, an idea snapped into his brain.

The lighter. He'd brought it along to use when he lit the joint. *You wanted her to smoke the joint*, a voice in his head whispered. He pushed the thought aside and pawed through his pocket.

Jace dropped the lighter into his lap and wiped his sweaty fingers on the front of his shorts. The last thing he needed was for the lighter to slip out of his grasp in the dark. Jace held the flame to the rope and tilted his chin so he could watch as the cord turned brown.

The smell reminded him of the cigarette Blyte had smoked. "Ha." The rope disintegrated faster than he'd imagined.

Within seconds the cord fell and one side of the noose was free. Jace could hear the blood whooshing in his ears. With only one length of rope holding him, there was room to manoeuvre. He stood and took hold of the remaining cord. The lighter felt hot in his hand. When he spun the wheel, he could feel the skin on his thumb burn. Gritting his teeth, he held the lighter to the last piece of rope.

Finally free from the long cords attached to the trees, but with the noose still tight around his throat, he shoved the lighter back in his pocket and stuck his injured thumb in his mouth. The car was out of the question: Blyte had taken the keys. The poker was gone, Blyte again. Jace listened for voices, but aside from the constant hiss of insects and endless croaking of unseen frogs, there was nothing.

As far as he knew, Cat and Eli were still inside the house so that's where he'd start. Blyte said he wasn't a killer and for some reason, Jace believed him. He also believed what he'd said about Felix. From the moment they had found him in the cellar, the guy had grated on Jace. Listening to Felix tell his story left Jace feeling like he'd watched someone acting in a rehearsed way. He had been trying too hard to be genuine, all the while snatching looks at people's faces. Maybe the best thing for everyone would be for Eli, Cat and Jace to walk away and let Blyte take care of Felix.

Still with no clear plan outside of reasoning with Blyte, Jace headed for the front of the house. *What about the shot?* The question kept bouncing around in his brain. As much as he tried to convince himself it was just an accident, a misfire, a crawling feeling in the pit of his gut made him pick up the pace.

Every few metres, he forced himself to stop and flick on the lighter. It slowed his progress but he didn't want to take the risk of running into another ambush. Blyte had already proved how lethal he could be. Next time Jace wanted to see him coming.

When he reached the corner of the building, he ducked into the bushes and flattened himself against the wall. Blyte was speaking again, his voice barely audible. He sounded softer, not so clipped. Jace stepped around the corner hoping to pick up what was being said. He could see Blyte's outline, it looked like he was pressed against the door.

A step closer and the words became clear. The hairs on Jace's arms stood up and the lighter slipped from his fingers. It couldn't be, the things Blyte said made no sense. Jace broke from the bushes, forgetting everything but reaching the door. He barrelled towards Blyte.

Chapter Twelve

Micky pressed his palms against the wood. The woman on the other side of the door was saying something but he couldn't quite make out the words. Her name was Caitlin, and by the sound of her voice she was terrified, but still holding it together.

"What? Caitlin, I can't hear you." He kept his tone calm, under control, even though it felt like his lungs were in a vice. If anything happened to her, it would be his fault. The last fifteen years had been about finding Amy, but now all he cared about was keeping a women he'd never even seen safe.

"I think he's coming." The fear in her voice hit him like a mallet.

He tried to think but his brain kept spewing up images of Amy. After all these years and so much planning, he was just as helpless as he'd been the day his sister disappeared.

"Hide." It wasn't much, but it was all he had to offer her. "Do you hear me, Caitlin? Hide." He jammed his shoulder against the door and shoved. Was it his imagination or did the heavy wood shift under his weight?

"I can't leave my husband." She wasn't whispering anymore. Her voice was raw with desperation.

"You can't help him if you're dead." Micky stopped shoving long enough to speak. "Go. Now. I'll get in somehow." He forced his mind to work through the layout of the house, searching for Caitlin's best option.

"But, I don't–"

"Upstairs. The last bedroom. You can get to the attic." He spat out a string of instructions praying there was still time. "Go!" He bellowed the last word and hoped it was enough to get her moving.

He pushed back, leaning out from the door. The upstairs lights were on. He could see a rectangle of light coming from the master bedroom. Would she have time to make it to the attic before Felix caught her? Micky pulled his gaze away and concentrated on the door.

Caitlin said she'd opened the bolt. He fished the keys out of his pocket and grabbed the penlight out of the waistband of his black jeans. Holding the light between his teeth, Micky inserted the key and listened as the lock snapped open. There'd been no point unlocking the door while the bolt was in place, but now the only thing standing between him and Felix was the furniture barricading the door. *That, and the gun.*

From what Caitlin described, he was pretty sure they'd wedged the antique sideboard against the door. Micky ran his hand over the back of his neck. The sideboard was made of African blackwood, one of the heaviest woods in the world. He'd bought the piece because of the rich dark colour, only realising how heavy it was when it nearly crippled him and the delivery guy getting it in the house.

Thinking about the day the sideboard was delivered, the way the delivery guy strained and groaned lifting the oversized antique, gave him an idea. The kid he'd caught round the side of the house, Jace. He was a tradesman, pretty muscular too. Caitlin was his sister-in-law. Micky let out a long breath, the girl said her husband had been shot, Jace's brother.

"Damn." None of this should have happened. Why the hell didn't he fit an alarm system in the house? *Because I didn't want to risk Felix getting loose and setting it off.* Micky had been so sure he could handle Felix, get the truth out of him when no one else could. *I wanted to hurt him with no one around to stop me.*

Blaming himself wouldn't help Caitlin. The best thing he could do for her now was to untie Jace and let him help get the door open. With the two of them pushing, they'd stand a better chance of getting through.

He pulled his key out of the lock and stuffed it back in his pocket. Just as he took a step away from the entrance, a sound caught his attention. Metal on metal, scraping. Micky ran at the door, using his shoulder as a battering ram. The wood shuddered as a stab of pain radiated through his arm.

"Too late, Micky." He'd only spoken to Felix Holly a handful of times over the last fifteen years, but Micky would recognise his voice anywhere. "You never should have brought me here." There was laughter in his tone. He was enjoying himself. "Without my medication, I do terrible things."

Micky gave the door another shove, knowing it was useless. "If you hurt them, I'll kill you." How many times had he threatened Felix with death over the last two days? No matter what Micky said, Felix just shook his head or laughed in his face. It was as if the man didn't understand *or* care about life or death. *Maybe he just knows I don't have the stomach for killing.* A creature like Felix would have a sixth sense for that sort of thing. He knew Micky couldn't take the ultimate step.

"I don't care what it takes." Micky's heart raced. "I'll get in there and tear you limb from limb if I have to." He thumped the side of his fist against the door in frustration. "Do you hear me?" He was roaring now, all control gone.

"You're never leaving here. I'll bury you and dance on your grave."

"Look what you made me do." Felix sounded farther away.

A shot, like a whip-crack, cut through the night. Micky's knees buckled.

Chapter Thirteen

Micky's voice broke through the fear. Caitlin pulled away from the door and stumbled towards her husband. His chest rose and sank with shallow breaths. Micky was right, she couldn't help him if she stayed. The only way to help Eli was to get them both out of the house.

Her mind felt muddy, as if sinking in a turbid pool of despair. The only way to break the spell was movement. She forced her legs to work, stepping past the blood, now cooling into a dark oily puddle on the floor. A whipping noise from the kitchen told her the extension cord was loose. She kicked off her tennis shoes knowing they were wet with blood and would leave a clear trail.

The stone, icy under her soles, helped shock her to focus on the moment and resist the urge to panic. She bolted for the stairs, flying upwards at a dizzying pace. Below, a crash that sounded like a tree falling. *He's out.* The realisation threatened to paralyse her, but Caitlin kept running.

There was no planning. She acted on instinct. At the door to the room she was to share with her husband, Caitlin paused. Her hands still bloody from the glass cuts and Eli's wound, she slapped her palm on the spotless white door. Tiny spikes of pain flared as the shards of glass bit deeper into her flesh making her gasp. She grabbed the knob.

What did Micky say? Something about the attic. She tried to put his words in order, but the sound of her breathing and the thudding of her heart blocked the memory. There was no time to hesitate. Her thoughts kept coming back to the linen cupboard. Inside the wall where she found the gun. A good hiding place.

She darted down the walkway. Before touching the door, she lifted the hem of her dress and used it to cover the handle. The fabric slipped, refusing to grip. How long would it take Felix to make it through the main room and up the stairs? By the time he got near the top, she'd be clearly visible—an easy shot. The act of clamping the dress around the knob took gargantuan effort, her fingers slipping like clumsy sausages. *Please, please.* She had no idea who or what she begged.

The handle moved and the door opened with a whisper. She snatched a blanket from the top shelf, again pulling down a jumble of towels. In the silence, the sound of feet slipping over carpet approached. Caitlin's heart thudded like a wild animal trapped in her chest.

She bent and pulled the false panel away from the wall and laid it flat on the floor. Climbing backwards into the cupboard and folding herself under the bottom shelf was easier than she'd thought. Apart from a bump to the back of her head, tucking into the small space was effortless. *Or I'm so scared I can't feel the pain.*

Curled on her left side, Caitlin covered herself with the blanket. Closing the door presented more of a problem. Getting it near closed was easy enough, but fully closed proved to be tricky. Running out of time, she finally hooked two fingers under the bottom of the door and pulled it closed.

A thin bar of light shone under the door, just enough illumination for her to pull the towels out from under her arm and arrange them in front of her face. If Felix opened the cupboard, the linen would disguise her presence, but only at first glance. She prayed it would be enough.

With the towels over her face, Caitlin lay in blackness. The odour of dust mixed with detergent filled her mouth and nose. Closing her eyes, she tried to focus on sound, but in the dark all she could see was Eli: bleeding and helpless. *I abandoned him.* In her mind, his face blurred and changed into that of a young girl. *I abandoned her too.* She'd left her husband lying in a pool of blood and fled. Whatever he'd done, the lies and indifference, he didn't deserve to die alone. Neither of them deserved that.

Banging. Even draped in fabric inside the cupboard, she could hear the sound coming from the front of the house. Micky said he'd get in, maybe he was pushing the sideboard out from behind the front door. Her heart still raced, but now with the possibility of rescue adding to the fear.

The seconds ticked by. The walls felt closer as if the cupboard shrank around her. Her bent legs ached, half-pushed into the small alcove where the gun had been hidden. She needed to stretch, work the cramp out of her thighs. *It's only been seconds, I can do this.* She tried to talk herself through the panic twisting in her stomach like a nest of worms. Why did she choose the cupboard? Small dark places filled her with dread, ever since… She sucked in a breath and felt the towel press against her lips. Letting her thoughts run wild would tug her into darkness. She couldn't let that happen, not now.

The thunderclap came so suddenly, Caitlin jumped, her head whacked the wall. For a second, dizzy and confused, she thought the sound was the cupboard door being torn off its hinges. A second later, the reality of what she heard sank in. A gun shot. Strangely, her first thought was of Micky. Had Felix shot him? The thought tore the air out of her lungs. Then, her panicked mind turned to Eli and she felt a rush of shame.

Muffled voices, more thumping. Caitlin thought of pushing the cupboard door open and trying to hear what was being said, but her hands remained clamped to her chest. At least in the cupboard she was safe. *Am I?* What if she opened the door and found Felix standing over her? The upstairs carpet was thick and soft, he could sneak up on her and she'd never hear him coming. But how long could she stay hidden?

The tumult of shouting and banging ceased. Caitlin realised her fists were bunched under her chin, pressing into her throat. In the silence, her breathing seemed thunderous, amplified by the silence, calling out to be discovered. She forced her fingers to uncurl and slapped a hand over her mouth.

"Here kitty-kitty." The words rose and fell in a singsong rhythm, tearing at Caitlin's nerves. When the gun went off, she'd hoped that somehow Felix was the one hit. But his was the only voice.

He sounded close. But swaddled in towels at the bottom of the cupboard, it was difficult to tell. She heard doors opening, something smash as if thrown against a wall.

"I know you're here, Kitty Cat." His voice was high, excited. He was enjoying himself. "There's nowhere to go."

Felix was right, she was caught like an animal in a trap. Tears filled her eyes and spilled over, falling sideways across the bridge of her nose. She could feel a sob building in her chest, the pressure of it burned her throat. Fear and lack of air pushed down on her until she thought she'd scream.

"I think I know where you're hiding." He gave a snorting laugh. "Not very bright, Kitty Cat." He sounded closer. Caitlin closed her eyes. "You really hurt me with that glass. I'm going to teach you a lesson."

I'm going to teach you a lesson. It was as if he'd reached into her soul and pulled a moment from its darkest depths.

Two voices raised in song. *I'm going to teach you a lesson. A lesson in love. Lo—ve.*

* * *

Trees, bathed in sunlight. Golden rays haloed Sharon's long yellow hair. She laughed, a light musical sound. "When we get to my place, I'll ask Mum if you can stay for dinner."

Caitlin let her head fall back against the seat. They were lucky to get a lift from Mr Campson before he left the Civic Centre. If he hadn't offered to drop them off, they'd be stuck waiting for the bus and Caitlin didn't want to waste a moment. Saturdays were her favourite, not just because she got to play netball. She loved being on the team, but the best part was after the game. Sharon always asked her over for dinner and sometimes Caitlin would be allowed to sleepover. Those were the best nights. Sharon's mum usually let them stay up watching DVDs in their games room. Around midnight she'd tell them to get their bums into bed and Sharon's dad would always yell for her to let the girls have ten more minutes. But he wasn't drunk or angry like the guys her mother brought home, just sort of funny and serious at the same time. He reminded Caitlin of the dads on TV. Normal. Nice.

"I'll have to ring and check if it's okay." If her mother was still hungover, she'd most likely get mad and say no. If she was still drunk, on a binge, she wouldn't answer the phone.

"I can get my mum to talk to her." Sharon was so pretty. Everyone at school wanted to be around her, but she chose Caitlin. If part of Sharon's friendship was based on pity, Caitlin didn't care. It was enough to have a friend who didn't judge her limited, scruffy wardrobe or the fact that she never had anyone to her house.

"This isn't the way." Sharon leaned forward and tapped the back of the front seat. "Mr Campson, this isn't the right way." She turned and looked out the rear window. "You missed the turn."

For a moment he didn't answer, his bald head gleamed like a pink gibbous moon above the headrest. Sharon, still leaning forward glanced over her shoulder and stared at Caitlin, giving her friend a wide-eyed look of confusion.

"Mr Campson?" Caitlin joined Sharon on the edge of the seat. In that moment, with both of them leaning forward, shoulders touching, Caitlin felt a tiny spark of worry.

"I've just got to make a quick stop." He didn't turn around. "There's something I want to show you girls." His voice was relaxed, almost dreamy. It reminded her of the way her mother sounded when she talked about her days at university.

"We really should—"

"It's not far. You like horses, don't you?" He turned and looked over his shoulder. Caitlin noticed his brown eyes were lined with tiny red veins. "Only I promised a friend I'd feed his horse while he's away. Thing is," he turned back to the road. His hands looked huge resting on the steering wheel, there was grime under his nails. "She's got a foal and won't let me near her."

"Aw." Sharon sighed. "I wish I was allowed to have a horse."

Caitlin poked Sharon in the thigh making her friend jump and give her a questioning stare. Caitlin shook her head, and grimaced, but Sharon shrugged. When Caitlin looked back to the front of the car, she caught him watching them in the rear-view mirror. Even though she knew he couldn't see her legs, she pulled on the hem of her netball skirt wishing she'd changed before Mr Campson offered them a lift. *He made it seem like he was in a hurry, that's why I didn't change.*

The car spun to the right and bumped onto a dirt track. They were at least ten minutes out of town. Trees and long bush-grass crowded the sides of the old station wagon. Caitlin remembered driving this way on a school trip to the dam. Only they'd been in a bus, driving along a proper road.

"We told Sharon's mum we would be home by lunchtime. She'll get worried if we're late." It was a lie, but Caitlin didn't feel guilty. She could see Sharon turning her head from side to side, checking both sides of the car. *She's looking for horses. I hope there's horses.*

"We won't be long." Was it her imagination or did his voice sound different?

Something solid hit the car's undercarriage, bouncing them up in their seats. Caitlin clenched her hands into fists and held onto the edge of the seat. There were no fences or houses this far east. Sharon turned her attention from the windows and met Caitlin's gaze. Her friend's eyes were shiny with tears. Sharon's hand found hers and curled over her fingers.

"Caitlin's right, Mr Campson. My mum *will* be worried." Her voice cracked. "I think you'd better take us back now." She squeezed Caitlin's hand.

"Yeah. I want to go back." Caitlin tried to make her voice sound stronger than she felt. "Or… or let us out here and we'll walk."

"It's just around this bend." He ignored their pleas. "What was that song you two were singing?"

"It's…it's…" Sharon was crying now. Her face, usually tanned, looked bleached of colour except for the red blotches forming on her cheeks. "It's *Lesson in Love* by Gracie Bliss."

There's two of us. He won't do anything. But wasn't that why they'd been so quick to accept his offer of a ride? There were two of them. They knew him because he worked at the Civic Centre where they played netball. He even got ice for Sharon's knee last year when she strained it. He was old. All the reasons why getting in his car had been no big deal, now seemed dumb. Dangerous.

"There it is." The car rolled to a stop. "Out." He didn't sound relaxed or dreamy. Mr Campson's voice was loud and hard. It made Caitlin's stomach flip over.

He opened the door and after a couple of grunts, pulled himself out. Once free of his weight, the station wagon bounced. Caitlin grabbed Sharon's netball shirt. "When we get out, run." She spoke quickly making sure he couldn't hear.

"What do you think he's—"

The back door creaked open. "Out." Mr Campson leaned in giving them a blast of stale breath. His eyes were like brown rocks at the bottom of a polluted pond. He sounded angry, like they'd done something wrong.

They didn't run. Campson walked behind the girls as they stumbled through the tangled weeds towards a black arc. The cave jutted out of a small hillside like an open mouth. Caitlin could hear his work boots crunching over the forest debris. They were in an isolated area. Judging by the clusters of dented cans, empty bottles and shell casings, it was some sort of hangout.

As they neared the mouth of the cave, Sharon began to sob. Caitlin took her hand, it was hot, shaking. "Don't leave me," Sharon's voice was small, like a little girl.

"Mr Campson we don't want to—"

"Shut up."

When they reached the cave, Caitlin turned to look at him and instantly regretted it. He was sweating, dark circles stained the sides of his blue work shirt. His mouth hung open like he was out of breath, revealing yellow teeth bunched together like the weeds that grew around the cave. Why had she never noticed how big and dirty he looked?

"Why do you wear those short little skirts?" His lower jaw moved when he spoke making him look like a puppet. "Is it because you want men to look at you?"

Sharon whimpered. Over his shoulder, golden sunlight played across the expanse of bush grass. Caitlin imagined herself running through the grass, her legs moving so swiftly they were a blur. She wanted to bolt, but her body wouldn't respond. Every muscle in her legs itched with the urge to run yet she was frozen.

"Get in there." He motioned to the cave.

"Please." Sharon squeezed Caitlin's hand so hard it felt like the bones would snap.

Campson took a step towards them, his hands bunched into fists. The girls stumbled back and turned to the cave. The smell of dirt and urine clogged Caitlin's mouth and nose. The walls were plastered with graffiti, the floor grey dirt. The sound of Campson's laboured breathing bounced around them as if he were everywhere. The ceiling was low, pressing down on her as if she were being buried. Caitlin felt a scream building in her chest like a hurricane.

* * *

The cupboard door swung open, snapping her back into the moment with jarring clarity. Light filtered through the towels blocking her face. He'd found her. Any second now, Felix would grab her by the shoulders and drag her out of the linen cupboard. Then it would all start again. She'd be fourteen, helpless—sobbing.

The door slammed shut. She didn't dare breathe until the sound of bare feet whispering over carpet told her he'd moved on. How had he missed the noise her heart made against her ribcage?

"I'm not enjoying this game anymore, Kitty Cat," his voice moved away. Was he going back to the bedroom?

She let out a shuddering breath. How long would it be before he came back and took another look? She had to move, get to the attic. At least up there, she might have a chance. As if hearing her thoughts, his bare feet padded back to the linen cupboard.

"Look, I'm not going to do anything to you. I told you before, you're too old from my tastes." His voice rose and fell as if he were pacing.

She was bathed in sweat now, struggling to stifle her panicked breathing. Something brushed her calf. When she found the gun, there had been cobwebs but no spiders. Maybe whatever spun the web had been hiding under the shelf. As horrifying as it was, the small dark space had been almost bearable, until the possibility of spiders entered her mind.

"I just need you to come outside with me. Micky and Dumbo won't try anything if you're with me." His voice grew louder, closer. "Once we get to the car, that's it. I'll let you go."

The brush on her calf turned into a tickle. A black hairy leg exploring her skin? A tremor ran through her body. She clamped her teeth together in an effort to suppress the movement.

"This is all just a big misunderstanding." He was farther away, she could tell by the muffled quality of his voice. "I promise, I'll let you go."

Part of her wanted to believe his lies. Anything to be free of the feeling of tiny legs crawling over her skin. But the look she'd seen in Felix's eyes told her a different story. She'd seen that look before, a mixture of anger and greed, with one fuelling the other. That look didn't lie.

She heard a crash as if a door had been flung open. He'd gone back to the bedroom, maybe planning on another search. Her mind cleared long enough to remember Micky telling her she could reach the attic through the last bedroom. Ignoring the feathery movement on her leg, Caitlin closed her eyes and pictured the upstairs layout. An L-shaped walkway. Doors on one side. Linen cupboard, last door on the left. She could see the door as clearly as if she were standing before it. Another door, not to the side but facing out.

Caitlin opened her eyes. The last bedroom was only a few metres from where she lay. Felix was still crashing around in the other room, searching. If she moved, there might be time to get to the other room before he came back. Caught in a tangle of indecision, her mother's words came back to her. *You show them what you can do.* What other choice did she have?

Pulling the towels off her face and untangling her legs took less than a second. The riskiest moment would be when the door opened. She'd be on the floor, vulnerable. In the seconds it would take her to stand, Felix could be on top of her. *I've done harder things.* Nodding her head, Caitlin pressed her fingers against the bottom of the door and pushed.

Chapter Fourteen

"You're never leaving here. I'll bury you and dance on your grave." Jace heard the words coming out of Blyte's mouth and the world narrowed. He couldn't think beyond what the man was roaring at his brother. At Caitlin.

His family were the target of Blyte's rage, it didn't matter what the man told him, as far as Jace was concerned, Blyte had to be stopped. Jace pumped his legs picking up speed. He'd take Blyte down and put an end to the games.

Without the lighter, the world pitched back into darkness. Another shot rang out, somehow louder in the blackness. Jace felt the strength go out of his legs and he stumbled. He hit the ground chest first with the metallic twang of the gunshot still reverberating in his ears. For a second his mind misfired and he thought the bullet had hit him. He only realised the shot came from inside the house in the seconds that followed.

Nothing made any sense. He scrambled to his feet and found himself caught in the blue-white brightness of Blyte's torch. Jace raised an arm to block the glare. "What the hell is going on?"

"Is the back door locked or just barricaded?" The question took Jace by surprise. It wasn't what he was expecting.

His mind jumped from the sound of the gunshot to Blyte's question and then back to what he'd heard the man screaming. "Who's shooting?" Jace wanted to ask more but his lungs were struggling to keep up.

"We need to get in. Felix has the gun." Blyte pulled the light off Jace's face and pointed it at the door. "It's bolted shut. Can we get in round the back?"

Jace was still processing what Blyte had told him when he turned and headed around the right side of the house. Jace bounded after him, eyes fixed on the torchlight as they tramped through damp grass.

"Wait. The shots, what happened?" He kept trying to put events in order. Blyte said Felix had the gun. There were two shots.

"I'm not sure who's been shot. We need to get inside." Blyte spoke over his shoulder. "Is the back door bolted, do you know?"

Jace followed Blyte trying to think back to the moment he slipped out the back door. He didn't remember anything about the bolt. When he and Eli shoved the fridge across the back door, they'd definitely bolted it. But, had Eli and Caitlin done the same?

His mind spun with questions as he watched Blyte stride around the rear of the house. For a few seconds, he was back in darkness. The world seemed much bigger at night, as if anything, even the unthinkable, were possible when the sun no longer shone. He turned the corner and spotted the light.

"Blyte." He jogged to keep up with him. "Did he shoot them?"

Blyte strode up the steps to the deck, not bothering to stop. "I told you, I don't know." His face was in profile, hidden by shadows. Even so, Jace had the feeling Blyte was hiding something.

He followed Blyte onto the deck and noticed his flip-flops at the top of the steps. How long had it been since he squeezed out the gap in the back door? An hour? He kept seeing his brother's face when he hit him. He could still feel the heat of the blow on his knuckles. *I should have never brought them here.*

"You're bleeding." Blyte shone the light on Jace's chest. "There."

Jace felt a moment's confusion then looked down at himself. There was a gash on his chest, just above the torn neckline of his t-shirt. Probably landed on a rock when he fell. He realised the noose still dangled from his neck.

"Here." Blyte took a step towards him. Instinctively, Jace stepped back. Blyte made a clicking sound with his tongue and took hold of the rope. "I'm surprised you got yourself out of this."

His fingers worked on the knot and in less than two seconds the rope dropped from Jace's neck. Jace ran his fingers around his throat feeling the raw, grazed skin. He felt lighter, as if the noose had compromised his breathing.

"Okay." Blyte turned and faced the door. "I'm guessing you barricaded the door with the fridge." Before Jace could ask how he knew, Blyte answered his question. "It would be my first idea." He pointed the light at the door. "We need to get this thing open. If the bolt's not in place, it should be manageable."

As desperately as he wanted to get in, Jace still had questions. "Did you talk to them? My brother and sister-in-law, are they okay?"

Blyte seemed lost in his examination of the door. When he finally answered, his words were clipped. "Spoke to the woman, not sure about your brother but…"

Jace's felt his muscles bunch as if his body expected a punch. "What about my brother?"

Blyte pulled his attention away from the door. He pointed the light down before he spoke so Jace couldn't see his expression. "He's been shot. Caitlin said he needed help so that tells us he's still alive, but we need to get inside before anyone else gets hurt."

Jace's head was nodding as if it worked independently of his body. Eli was shot. The words went through his brain, but he couldn't take in their meaning. In spite of the humidity in the air, his skin felt cold. How could any of this be happening? And beneath the shock, a shameful panicky squirm of guilt.

"I know you're shaken up, but we need to move." How could Blyte be so calm?

Jace knew he was to blame for what was happening to his family. For what *had* happened to his brother. He'd brought them here. He was the one who broke the law by copying the key and using the house, but didn't Blyte also own some of the guilt? He felt a jolt of anger towards the man. He had the firearm. He was the one who'd taken the law into his own hands and stuck Felix in the cellar.

"Yeah, let's go." Jace suppressed the urge to grab Blyte by the front of his shirt and slam him against the door, use *him* as a battering ram.

They stood side by side, with Blyte ahead of Jace. The torch, still on, protruded from the back of Blyte's pants like an eerie appendage. On Blyte's count, they pushed. The door, heavy and dark, almost identical to the one at the front of the building, refused to budge.

"It's not working." Jace used his shoulder, knees bent and pushed.

"It'll work." Blyte's voice was strained, like he was speaking through clenched teeth.

The tendons in Jace's neck pulled so tight, he thought they'd snap. His knees groaned under the strain. Just when he was about to pull back, the door shifted and started to slide.

"Wait." Blyte stood back and repositioned himself so his shoulder was higher up the panel.

Jace followed suit and both men rammed themselves at the door. Another few more centimetres and Jace could hear the fridge scouring across the stone. His shoulder and back burned with the effort. Sweat dripped off his hair in fat globs and ran into his eyes. Clamping his teeth together, he heaved once more and the door shifted.

Chapter Fifteen

Lights, dazzlingly bright—a blinding moment and then clarity. She'd been in the dark of the cupboard for what felt like hours, the glare took a few seconds to coalesce into actuality. Crawling commando style, elbow over elbow, Caitlin pulled herself out of the confinements of her hiding place. She could smell Felix's presence on the walkway, earthy and sour.

The door to the last bedroom stood ajar, directly to her left and only metres away. Still on her hands and knees, she turned and swung the cupboard behind her. It closed with a soft *click*. Caitlin froze and watched the hallway. A dull thud, as if something large had hit a wall, came from the bedroom Eli chose.

If Felix were still searching down the hall, she might have time to make it to the last bedroom before he returned. Her mouth felt dry, as if all the moisture had been sucked out of her body. One more glance down the hall, then she was moving.

She crossed the space in three strides, her feet sliding soundlessly over the plush carpet. She slipped her body through the dark opening. Again, her eyes took a moment to adjust. The lights were off in the room. The only illumination came from the walkway lights spilling through the thirty-centimetre opening, washing the room in fuzzy grey.

"Where the fuck are you?" Felix was back on the walkway. His voice an angry, almost feminine shriek.

Caitlin moved deeper into the room and eased her way behind the door. She could hear his feet scrape across the carpet, the *whoosh* of his clothes. Pressing a hand to her chest, she tried to calm the thumping that threatened to give her away. If he came into the last bedroom and turned on the light, she was done. There'd be nowhere to go.

He stopped near the door. Ragged breathing filled the darkness. Caitlin didn't dare blink. In her head, she counted off the seconds. After six, another rustle of fabric as he turned and walked away. Her knees trembled as she let out a long-held breath. *I can't relax, not even for a second.*

There was no way of knowing how near or far Felix might be lurking. She had only two choices: keep going or stand behind the door all night. *Micky said he'd get in.* She believed he would. A huge part of her wanted to stay rooted to the spot and wait for him to rescue her. But what if he couldn't get the door open? Or worse, what if Felix shot him? Now, like when she was fourteen, the only person she could depend on was herself.

Micky told her there was an access door in the ceiling, he even told her where to find the pole so she could hook the door open. The only problem was the lack of light. She could make out shapes, but without a little more illumination, it was almost impossible to find the door in the ceiling, let alone the pole.

Her only chance was more light. Caitlin inched forward until she was out from behind the door but still along the wall. Felix seemed to be pacing like a caged lion. Taking a look around the door would mean risking being spotted. She hoped luck was on her side and he was pacing away from the door. After a moment's hesitation, she jutted her head forward and peered out.

Felix was nowhere in sight and there were faint bloody marks on the carpet leading from the cupboard to the last bedroom. *Oh Christ.* How had he not noticed the marks? Her luck wouldn't hold, it was now or never. Caitlin swallowed and pulled the door open a little further. She swivelled her head, checking the ceiling.

"Yes." The word came out before she could stop herself. Only a whisper of sound but to her ears, shockingly loud.

No matter, she'd spotted the access door and the ring. If she moved fast, she could be in the attic before he came back. *You don't know that.* No, in truth she had no idea how long Felix would wander before returning. But dwelling on the possibility of being seen wouldn't help her with what she had to do.

With the extra light, she could see the bed in sharper detail. Trying to keep close to the far wall and out of the doorway, Caitlin crossed the small room and dropped down. She got another waft of dust, this time mixed with nylon from the carpet. Chest pressed to the floor, she extended her right arm and began patting the area under the bed. Within seconds, her fingers found the pole.

The urge to laugh out loud swept over her. If her mouth wasn't so dry, she might have given in and chuckled. Finally, things were going the right way. Caitlin scrambled to her feet and raised the pole above her head. Her heart hammered, now with a mix of excitement and fear. *Better than just fear.*

She took a few steps to the right and swiped at the ring, missing by at least ten centimetres. *Damn.* Standing just out of the sweep of light from the door, she raised the pole over her head for another try. If Felix came back down the walkway, he'd have to turn just before the linen cupboard and then the last bedroom would be in sight. With the door further open, he might spot her even in the shadows.

Stop it. Don't think about him. Focus. Arms trembling above her head, Caitlin took another swipe at the hook. Her dress flapped against her body like a damp sack. She could smell herself, bathed in sweat and blood. Maybe he'd catch her scent before he even saw her? The pole swayed just beside the ring and then caught.

This time she did laugh, a dry, brittle sound barely strong enough to make it past her throat. One firm tug and the access flap turned down. A set of aluminium steps unfolded with a gassy exhale followed by a metallic *clang*. Caitlin couldn't resist snatching a look towards the door.

"I can hear you." Felix's voice rang out. "Stupid bitch." He sounded close.

Caitlin sprang on the ladder, arms and legs spread like a spider monkey. Still clutching the pole, she clamoured up the rungs praying her legs didn't choose this moment to give out. Once at the top, she stepped into darkness, dropped the pole then turned and grabbed the ladder's side rail. The fold-out structure jumped but remained in place.

"Oh God." Caitlin leaned out of the roof space until her head almost touched the metal rungs. The light snapped on, its glare jarring and sudden. Felix stood in the doorway, gun at his side and mouth open in a black circle of shock.

Hanging out of the ceiling gave her the extra reach she needed to grab the side-rail lower and get a better swing. This time when she pulled, the ladder contracted and slid upwards with a series of clanging snaps. Felix's face appeared below, a look of panic on distorted his features. He opened his mouth but his words were cut off by the slap of the access door slamming shut.

Caitlin held the side-rail, crouched low and panted. Felix screamed abuse from below, but the sound was muffled. Any relief she felt was swallowed up by the knowledge that he wouldn't give in until he caught her. *And then what?* Why didn't he just go? Surely after what

Micky did to him Felix would want to get as far away from the house as possible. Why hang around? Why keep after her? Maybe he could tell she was damaged goods? *Maybe he can smell it on me, what Campson did.*

Staring wide-eyed into the darkness, desperate to make some sense of her surroundings, something brushed her cheek. She thought of the cupboard, the feeling of something crawling on her skin. Still holding the handrail as if it was the only thing that anchored her in the blackness, Caitlin shrieked and swatted at her face. Her fingers touched something cold, it disappeared and then hit her cheek a second time. A cord. Grasping blindly, she took hold of the swinging cord and pulled.

Pale, almost blue light shone down illuminating the access panel and glinting off the folded ladder. Caitlin's first thought was the pole. She looked around her knees and to her right, spotting it just out of reach. Only daring to let go of the handrail for a second, she reached over and grabbed the pole. Micky had given her hurried instructions on how to get into the attic, but nothing on how to secure the hatch once she was in.

Even without the pole, Felix could find something to stand on and hook his finger through the ring. As the thought ran through her mind, a rumble came from below. He was moving the bed, she was sure of it. Caitlin did the only thing she could think of to keep him out; she shoved the pole through the handrail. The pole was longer than the width of the opening, wedged across the rail it would prevent the hatch from being pulled down.

A scratching at the access flap and the distinct sound of the ring rattling shattered her last nerve. Caitlin leaned back on her haunches and pressed her fists against the sides of her head. Why didn't he just go? Her body felt heavy, slack and used up as if the constant fear had sucked every ounce of strength from her muscles. She didn't have much more to give. The access flap jumped, rattling the pole. He was trying to get in.

"Just go." She leaned down and screamed, "Just go! Go!" Her voice rasped, cracking with desperation.

For a second there was no response. She allowed herself to hope, maybe he'd heard her and decided to give up. To her left, a chunk of ceiling exploded with and earsplitting crack, sending fragments of plaster and wood in all directions. Stinging heat tore through her ear. The suddenness of the shot and the pain set her off balance.

She fell to the right and forced her body to roll, trying to put some distance between her and the splintered patch of ceiling. She had to move, get away from the access flap. Caitlin pressed a hand to her injured ear and managed to get her legs under her. The attic was little more than a crudely put together loft space. A large expanse of beams laid over with planks. At the far-left end, a window.

Moving slowly, trying to minimise the sound her bare feet made on the boards, she headed for the window. If she got to the far end, she'd be away from the last bedroom, maybe over the master bedroom. The important thing was not making any noise. If Felix didn't know what part of the roof she was in, he wouldn't be able to take shots at her.

The air in the attic was stifling and heavy with dust. A few tins of paint and some carpet off-cuts were the only items she could see. Caitlin reached the window and sank down with her back to the wall still holding her ear. How long had it been since she'd last sat? It seemed like she'd been on the run for hours. Her limbs felt battered, her right leg throbbed, and her ear burned as if it had been scalded. Gingerly, she let go of her ear, wincing as the air touched the wound. Her fingers were sticky with blood. She risked exploring the damage and discovered a hunk of what she guessed was splintered wood protruding from the top of her ear like a jagged earring.

A wave of wooziness swept over her and the attic dimmed. She pulled her fingers away and drew in a deep breath through her nose. An old mantra sprang to mind, something she learned in high school health class. *Smell the rose and blow out the candle.* Deep breathe in through the nose and out through the mouth. She repeated the process, taking in a long breath and then letting it out again. The dizziness faded. Her mind began conjuring up images of what the wound might look like, but she quickly shut off the thoughts.

Caitlin examined her leg, unsure why it felt so warm and heavy. What she found was more disturbing than the splinter sticking out of her ear. On the outside of her calf, two red welts, each about the size of a pea with a bruised spot in the centre. Her mind jumped back to the cupboard. The crawling feeling on her skin. The evil looking twin marks on her skin left her in no doubt a spider had not only crawled over her leg, but had bitten her. She shuddered and let out a whimper. As if the night wasn't horrendous enough.

A ripple of nausea stirred in her gut. Spider venom going to work on her or a physical reaction to the thought of a bite? She didn't know what to think, all she knew was that when she thought things couldn't get any worse, somehow they did. Without actually seeing the spider, she had no way of knowing how serious the bite might be. A Huntsman spider had large powerful fangs but was harmless enough—usually. Her mind threw up an image of another spider, shiny body, inky black with a distinctive red dorsal stripe. If it was a Redback, she might be in real trouble.

She ran her hand through her hair and gasped as her palm flicked her ear. A new rush of tears filled her eyes. "Micky, you said you'd come."

Caitlin let her face fall into her hands. Deep exhaustion engulfed her, sucking every drop of determination from her body. With the immediate danger on hold, she felt her mind slip into numbness. A numbness starting with her thoughts and spreading to her nerves and bones. She had no desire to fight the feeling, not for a while at least.

Chapter Sixteen

Blood covered his hands. Felix tucked the gun into the waistband of his pants, and held them up to the light. For a moment, he lost himself. *Levelling out*, that's how he saw the chunks of time when his brain stuttered to a halt. Felix stared at the blood, it looked almost too bright under the light. His blood, spilled by the bitch.

He'd been off his meds for almost three days. His thoughts were sharper now. He could hear himself think. The thoughts exquisite, the memories tantalising. Except for—his mind halted. Blyte's face ballooned in his brain. A spectre dogging his steps; if not for the meds, Felix would never have allowed himself to be cornered—tricked. He rubbed his hands on the front of his shirt leaving smears of blood mingled with grime.

So many years spent in a cocoon of need. The meds were supposed to take away the impulses that gnawed at him, but instead, the pills made him helpless. The nurses at the hospital treated him like a child. Not with kindness, but disgust. He could see the loathing in their eyes even as they pretended to understand. He'd been living a half-life, never at peace, always needing the satisfaction that no one could understand. His thoughts turned to Uncle Howie; he understood. Uncle Howie knew they were just men following their instincts, no worse than... His thoughts faded. The pale walls reminded him of Graylands, for an instant he thought he was back in hospital.

Felix tapped his finger on the swelling below his eye. A splinter of pain jabbed at his face, clearing his thoughts. Levelling out the doubts. He was in Blyte's house and there was work to do. Blyte and the two brothers, were like the nurses; simple-minded and brutish. They thought they'd cornered him, but he'd show them.

"A quick stop." His voice was calm, almost cheerful as he pushed open the door to the master bedroom. Locating the items he needed took less than a minute. "What a dump." He remembered the line from an old movie and chuckled. He really had made a mess of the room.

He shouldn't be angry, not really. Blyte did him a favour in a way. Jumping him outside of the local swimming pool, bringing him here had, in many ways, set him free. Countless days spent wandering, watching but powerless to plan or act. All that was over now. After tonight, he'd start again. The lessons he learned last time, with Amy, would make him cautious.

Amy. With the haze lifted, he could remember his time with her. Not the first, but to his mind the best of his girls. Felix reached the end of the walkway. Absently, without even thinking, he shambled to the stairs. Blyte's face appeared in his mind, souring the image he'd been enjoying. *So desperate to know.* He snorted. All the pleading and the beating. Felix felt a buzz of pride. He didn't break. He'd never break.

"It won't be long now, Micky. You'll see her soon." He headed down, drips of blood, warm and sticky ran down his stomach, dripping from the hem of his shirt. His spirits were high. So high he wanted to sing. The words popped into his head. He remembered hearing the children at Storytime at his local library singing it. There was nothing more enjoyable than Storytime. He frowned. *Until that bloated cow librarian gave me the evil eye.* He pushed the unpleasant thoughts away and started singing, softly at first but then with gusto.

"When all the hens were roosting and the moon behind a cloud, up jumped a scarecrow and shouted very loud." He walked towards the front door, gun dangling at his side, a woman's white t-shirt slung over his shoulder and a bedspread tucked under one arm. The sound of pounding came from the back door.

"Time to make myself scarce." He spoke to the empty sitting room and then continued singing. As he walked towards Eli's lifeless body, Felix paused and bent over the dead man. "Up jumped a scarecrow and shouted very loud."

Chapter Seventeen

"Wait." Micky pulled back from the door. "Did you hear that?" He took another backwards step.

"Hear what?"

Micky ran to the edge of the deck and jumped. The light was on in the attic, spilling out an eerie blue-white glow. *She made it.* A weight, like a sack of cement on his chest, lifted. He'd only spoken to Caitlin for a few minutes, but there was a sadness in her voice that he knew was in his own. Always there, underlying everything he said and did.

"What is it?" Jace stood by the door, his face in shadows.

Micky pointed up. "Your sister-in-law. I told her to get up to the attic. Light's on." In spite of the situation, he couldn't help grinning. "She did it."

A shot rang out. This one closer, overhead. Blyte leapt back onto the deck and ran at the door. "We need to get in. Now."

Another shove and the door moved inwards. Jace pulled back and turned so he was side on. He tried to slide his large frame through the gap. Micky watched him knowing there wasn't enough room. He was desperate.

Micky couldn't blame him. His brother was in the house, maybe dying as they struggled to get the door open.

"Keep pushing." He tried to think of something comforting, but came up empty.

Jace wedged his arm around the door and his right leg through the gap. He grimaced and clamped his teeth together. Micky waited while the other man squirmed and pushed. Finally, Jace pulled back from the gap. He stooped over and braced his hands on his knees, panting with exhaustion.

When Jace looked up, his face was pale and bathed in sweat. "It's my fault they're in there."

Micky couldn't argue. The kid shouldn't have stolen the key and copied it. It was a dumb thing to do, but maybe Micky should have been more careful. He should have never left Felix in the cellar and gone into Mandurah. What was he thinking? *I wasn't thinking. I've been blind with hatred for so long, I stopped thinking about anything else but finding Amy.* But was that really what he was trying to do? He realised the quest had become more about punishing Felix than helping his mother find closure. Everything else came second to his obsession, even finding his little sister.

"We've all done stupid things." He thought of clapping Jace on the shoulder, but the idea seemed forced—awkward. "Let's try and put something right." He jerked his chin towards the door.

Jace nodded and straightened up. "Yeah. Right."

They worked on the door, with each centimetre the heavy wood moved, they took turns trying to fit through the gap. After a few more minutes, Micky sucked in a breath and squeezed into the gap. To his surprise, his body slipped through and he found himself in the kitchen.

He turned and spoke to Jace through the gap. "I'll try and shift the fridge from in here." He was whispering now, aware that Felix was armed and could be anywhere. While his training told him to be cautious, Micky had a gut feeling that told him a coward like Felix Holly would prefer sneaking around to a front-on assault—at least when it came to dealing with another man and not a woman or child.

"Do you see them?"

Micky could only see one side of Jace's face. The torch light washed his skin in blue making him look ghostly. "No. Nothing." Micky wiped his hands on his pants and stepped around the fridge.

The extension cord trailed from the sleek silver handle. He could see how Caitlin had rigged the cellar door to keep Felix trapped. He was struck by her inventiveness. There was a bloody handprint on the fridge—impossibly red against the white. A small hand. The sheen of sweat on his face grew cold on his skin, trickling down his neck like icy fingers. He'd seen a lot of blood during his time in the army, but nothing had ever chilled him as much as that single handprint.

"Blyte?" Jace's voice from the deck dragged his attention away from the blood.

"Right here," Micky called around the giant appliance. "I'm going to shut the back door and get behind the fridge, see if I can edge it out a bit further."

He closed the door and squeezed in behind the fridge. *What the hell was I thinking? Who needs a fridge this size?* He braced his hands on the maze of black metal that criss-crossed the back of the appliance and pushed. The white giant slid forward a few centimetres. He hoped it would be enough because he had a feeling they were running out of time.

This time, when Jace shoved his shoulder through the gap, the rest of his body followed. He started for the sitting room but Micky stopped him. "Wait. I need something first."

Jace shrugged. "So get it, I'm going to find Eli and Caitlin."

"No. Just give me a minute." Micky paused. He was telling the truth about needing to grab something, but he also didn't want Jace finding his brother alone. "I need you to watch my back while I do a bit of climbing."

Jace looked confused, but nodded. It was an impatient gesture. He looked over Micky's shoulder and his eyes widened. "Holy shit." Micky followed Jace's gaze. "Is that... is that a handprint?"

Micky left Jace staring at the fridge and dragged a stool over to the kitchen bench alongside the wall to the sitting room. He climbed up and opened the double doors on the top shelf. A row of eight wine glasses sat on the white laminate lining. Taking hold of the first and last glass, he lifted and pulled at the same time. The entire row came out in his hands, the glasses glued in place.

"You have got to be kidding." Jace spoke from below him. "Is that a false shelf?"

"Hold it for me, will you?" Micky handed down the shelf, complete with wine glasses. The dumbfounded look on the guy's face almost made Micky smile.

Jace held the false shelf, turning it side on so he could examine the base. Micky turned back to the cupboard and reached in with both hands.

"Jesus. Is that thing loaded?" Jace put the false shelf down on the stove-top and stared open-mouthed at the sleek black shotgun.

Micky jumped down from the stool holding the gun out in front of his chest. "It wouldn't be any good to us if it wasn't." He slung the strap over his shoulder. "Let's go."

Micky could smell the body before they got near the front door. The sickening mix of blood and deathly odours hit the back of his mouth. There was no stopping Jace, he darted forward and fell to his knees.

"Eli?" Micky watched the kid put his hands on his brother's chest as if he could shock the body back to life. "Eli." Jace's shoulders hunched, he lowered his head until it was nearly touching his hands.

Micky felt his gut tightening. He didn't want to watch, but found it difficult to pull his gaze away. They never found his sister. He didn't get the opportunity to say goodbye to her. The loss of what should have been his right weighed on him. It almost took his sanity. But watching Jace crouched over his brother's body, Micky wondered if he'd been better off.

Something caught his attention. Jace's brother had been shot twice, that was clear. Covered in a yellow blanket, a dark patch of blood had soaked through just below the left ribs. Judging by the size of the patch, the man had been alive and bleeding heavily when the blanket was put over him. What interested Micky was the head wound. He'd been shot at close range, just above the right eye. His right hand or what was left of it, lay on his chest, bent at an awkward angle. Micky was no expert, but it looked like the guy was not only alive when he was shot the second time, but conscious. *He raised his hand to try and block the bullet.*

Micky didn't think it possible to hate someone with more bitterness than he already did with Felix. He'd never met Jace's brother. That wasn't quite true, he'd spoken to the man through the door. Exchanged a few angry words. Yet the thought of him trying to block the shot, wounded and alone, stirred something dark and cold in Micky's heart. A need to hurt. A longing that could only be satisfied by violence.

He could hear Jace speaking, talking to his brother. The man's voice sounded hurried—pleading. Micky turned away not wanting to hear but unable to tune the words out. *I'm sorry, I should have been there.* How many times had he wanted to tell Amy those very words?

This was only the beginning. There would be years of guilt and grief ahead and in those long years, it would always come back to this moment. Jace would be a prisoner of this memory, maybe for the rest of his life.

He noticed blood, dropped in splatters on the stone floor. The trail led from the stairs to where Jace still crouched, now holding his brother's uninjured hand. For the first time since entering the sitting room, Micky realised the front door was open. He turned from the door and noticed a pair of black tennis shoes tossed to the side near the study.

"We need to find your sister-in-law." He sounded callous. Not how he wanted the words to come out. He wished he could take them back, think of a better way but tact had never been his talent. "We need to be careful, he could still be hiding up there."

Jace rocked back and forth. A slight movement, barely noticeable. He laid his brother's hand on the floor and pulled the blood-stained blanket up over his head. Micky was glad the man's face was covered so he didn't have to see the shock and confusion frozen into his features.

They moved upstairs, Micky in the lead. Jace hadn't spoken since they found the body. Grief and anger encased him like a nebulous cloud. Something invisible yet palpable. More blood on the carpet; it looked like someone had gone up and down the stairs bleeding profusely. The trail leading to the front door was either Felix's or Caitlin's. If it were Felix's, then he'd gone. As always, wreaked havoc and slipped away. As much as Micky wanted to turn and hunt the man down, what he really needed was to make sure Caitlin was safe. Everything else could wait.

The walkway was a maze of blood stains. Even though Micky had warned him, Jace pushed past and headed down the landing. "Which one leads to the attic?" He made no attempt at stealth. If Felix was up here, Jace had announced their presence.

Micky pointed to the door at the far end of the L-shape walkway. Jace stomped towards the last bedroom, head down like a charging bull. Micky watched him go, hanging back. He slipped the shotgun off his shoulder and disabled the trigger guard. If Felix came out of hiding, Micky wanted to be ready. He'd do what he should have done all along.

Jace slammed open the door at the far end of the walkway. Micky paused, listening for sounds of a struggle. Nothing. He pushed open the door to the master bedroom avoiding the smears of blood around the handle. The room had been torn apart, not just trashed, but decimated. Mattress tossed, clothes everywhere. The drawers on the dresser were hanging out, blood smeared on the walls. He'd always known Felix was sick. An evil mind hidden behind a mask of mild manners and mental illness, but the way the room was trashed showed signs of a fury that was almost diabolical. *Amy.* He thought of his little sister. What must her final moments have been like in the hands of someone capable of so much rage? Tears stung his eyes. Still gripping the shotgun, he wiped them on his shirt.

"Cat. Cat, are you there?"

Micky stepped out of the room and followed the sound of Jace's voice.

Chapter Eighteen

Sharon's skin, pale and flawless, had glowed in the dimness. So white against the dirty walls, she didn't seem real. Except for the look on her face. Her face made everything real. Breathing, whimpering, Campson grunting, the sounds of her friend's torture bounced off the walls. Caitlin clamped her hands to her ears trying to block out the noise. She could smell him, his slimy odour all over her.

The walls were damp and cold. The earth beneath her feet reeked of urine. Campson's back was to her. His blubbery body glistening with sweat. Over his shoulder she could see her friend's pleading look. Caitlin watched; cowered and watched. She wished she could tear him off Sharon, pull her friend free and together they'd run. In her mind, she could see herself doing it. Picking up the broken bottle. Walking across the cave and jamming it into the man's naked back.

The image snapping on and off like a photograph whirring through the wind. And still the incessant noises continued. Sharon's voice, begging, barely coherent. The pleas became frantic. Caitlin's heart kept time with the cries, all the while thankful Mr Campson was done with her and had turned his attention on her friend.

Make it stop. Make it stop. Caitlin tore her eyes away, unable to stand the look of pleading on her friend's face. The daylight at the mouth of the cave looked flat and impartial. Sharon screamed, an agonised sound bounced off the walls of the cave. The cry, so shrill, was cut off as suddenly as it began. Caitlin turned back and choked down her own scream.

Campson's hands were around Sharon's neck, squeezing and shaking the girl like a toy. *He's killing her.* Caitlin snatched another look at the outside world then back at the vile scene. *He'll kill me too.* Her legs wobbled and then moved. Stumbling at first, one hand on the wall, she made it to the mouth of the cave. She could hear Campson grunting, the noise surrounded her. Another two steps and she was almost in the light.

"Don't you move." He was breathing hard, as if he'd been running. His voice edged with violence. *He's out of breath.*

Caitlin half-fell, half-jumped into the light. When the sun hit her skin, it was as if she'd caught fire. Every nerve felt hot and alive. She ran, not picking up speed but unstoppable from the first step. Arms pistoning, torn netball jersey hanging from her shoulders and blood running down her thighs, she sprinted.

She veered away from the station wagon and ran towards the trees. *Don't look back.* She belted past a broken fencepost, a finger of rusty wire grabbed at what was left of her clothing pulling her shirt from her shoulders and still she kept running.

The ground sloped downwards careening her forward at an unrelenting pace. The sky seemed to pitch and she tumbled, legs and arms cartwheeling. When she landed, her chin smacked the ground with enough force to make her teeth clamp down on her tongue. The taste of blood filled her mouth but registered only as an afterthought.

Caitlin kept moving. Each step sent a jab of pain through her side. Her lungs felt hot, ready to explode. *Got to run. Don't look back.* Not until her feet hit the bitumen did she dare slow down. Only when the coarse uneven surface grazed her foot did she realise she'd lost a shoe. For some reason, the missing shoe tipped her over into exhaustion. Her knees hit the road. A flock of birds swarmed overhead. Screeching filled the air, blocking out the sound of the engine as it barrelled towards her.

Caitlin held up her hand, elbow jerking with the effort. The car screamed to a halt. Doors slamming. Voices. Questions. She felt herself being lifted under the arms and panic took hold.

"No. Please no." She heard herself crying, her voice barely recognisable as her own. She struggled, trying to pull free.

"It's okay, love. I just want to help." A woman's voice. *Not Campson*, but a woman. "Let's get you in the car." The voice was soft, soothing. Caitlin started to cry.

"I… I want to go home," the words tumbled out like a wail. "I just want to go home."

* * *

"Cat? Cat, are you there?"

She raised her head. For a moment, the past and present melded together. The cave. The attic. Her mind wavered between the two, before clearing. With clarity came panic. She had to get out, get help for Eli.

"Cat? Cat, it's Jace." The access flap jumped but the pole held.

Jace. She wanted it to be true so badly. But the dreams and memories were so real, was she dreaming now? Touching a finger to her ear, she gasped. The pain was real.

"Caitlin?" Another voice joined Jace's.

"I'm here." The words came out cracked, inaudible. She uncurled herself and scurried towards the flap on all

149

fours. The sudden movement sent searing pain through her calf. Her vision doubled and bile rose in her throat.

She swallowed and kept moving. "I'm here. I'm up here." The words were clear now. They'd found her. *Micky found her.* The nightmare was over.

Still on all fours, she slid the pole out of the handrail. Within seconds, a hydraulic *whoosh* and the flap opened. Jace's head appeared, his eyes only centimetres from hers. For a second, neither of them spoke. He looked pale, older somehow. *I bet I look like hell too.*

"Are you okay?" his voice rasped as if something stuck in his throat.

She wanted to speak, tell him of the horrors she'd been through. "Yeah. I'm okay."

Jace stayed behind her as she backed down the ladder. There were a few moments when her legs threatened to give out, but he was there ready to catch her. Once down, her thoughts were clearer, as if the stale, humid air in the attic had clouded her mind.

"You made it up there okay." Hands still braced on the ladder, she recognised the voice before turning around.

He wasn't what she'd been expecting. Tall but not overly so. Older than she imagined, early forties. Dark green eyes, the colour reminded her of an old wine bottle washed up on the beach. They were kind eyes that belied the muscular frame and the hard set of his mouth. She wondered briefly what it would be like to press her head against his chest and close her eyes.

"Just about." It was all she could manage. If she said more, the tears would start and she'd done enough crying to last a life-time. She turned to Jace. "We need to get Eli to a hospital."

Something passed between the two men. A look so swift, it might have been her imagination. Jace shifted his weight from one foot to the other as if trying to find his balance. The movement sent a wave of dread crashing against her already ragged nerves.

"Tell me." She looked at Micky, not sure why she expected only honesty from the man.

"Felix killed him... I'm sorry." His voice was flat, almost emotionless.

Her mouth was moving, she could feel her lips coming together and then parting. No words came out. *I left him. Left him to die, just like I did with Sharon.* She could see his wide confused eyes, it was as if Sharon and Eli occupied the same pleading gaze. Her legs felt weightless as if she were floating. Someone called her name and then the world went dark.

* * *

Jace's face hovered above her. "Cat." His features blurred then snapped back into place. "Don't try to sit up."

She ignored him and pulled herself into a sitting position. Something was different. She was in the sitting room, on the sofa with a dark-coloured wool blanket puddled in her lap. For a moment there was relief. She was out of the attic and Felix was gone. A split second of lightness, as if a boulder had been rolled off her back. But just as quickly reality hit her. Eli. Dead.

"Here." He handed her a bottle of water. "Drink."

She wanted to push the bottle away, but took it and made herself swallow. The cool liquid tasted clean on her parched tongue. She took another sip and thought of the way the cold water felt washing over her body only hours ago when the three of them swam in the river.

"He can't be—I can't believe it." She wanted to be wrong, maybe she'd dreamt it. The look in Jace's eyes was enough to confirm what she already knew to be true. "I'm so sorry, Jace."

He nodded, the muscles in his face moved as he tried to keep his emotions in check. She reached out and slipped her arms around his shoulders. He fell into her, his face hot against her neck.

"I'm so sorry." She repeated the words, not sure if she were talking to Jace or Eli.

After a moment that seemed endless and too fast at the same time, she pulled back. She turned to her left and tried to look over Jace's shoulder, searching for Eli's body. Her eyes found a snatch of yellow and her stomach lurched. The view was shut off by Micky's body.

"We need to decide what we're going to do now."

She noticed the shotgun slung over his shoulder and felt a quiver of fear.

"What do you mean?" She tried to drag her gaze away from the gun. It looked enormous and deadly.

"Felix is gone," Jace answered. "It looks like he went out the front." He seemed nervous, he hesitated and looked over his shoulder.

"We can get in the car and drive to Mandurah. Go to the police and let them sort all this out." Micky jerked his thumb towards the door.

It seemed like the logical thing to do, but she sensed there was something else. Something had been discussed while she was out. The quiver of fear she felt looking at the shotgun turned into a thick hand slapping at her insides.

"The cops will probably find him." Micky planted his hands on his hips. "They'll put him back in hospital. Pump him full of drugs and that will be the end of it. He'll never stand trial. Never answer for what he's done." She could hear the bitterness in his voice. "What he did to your husband. To my sister." He shrugged. "None of it will matter because he's too good at playing the game."

"What do you mean? What game?" Caitlin closed her eyes trying to make sense of what Micky was saying. Could it really be true? Felix would somehow get away with killing Eli?

"He's crazy. That part's true, but he's got the doctors convinced he's not capable of understanding what he's done." He rubbed his hand over the back of his neck. "I

152

don't know. He's been diagnosed with so many mental health issues, he'll never see the inside of a prison cell."

"So, what are you suggesting?"

"I can stop him. Put an end to it now. Tonight."

Caitlin wasn't surprised Micky wanted to kill the man responsible for murdering his sister. What did shock her was Jace's silence which she took as agreement.

"Jace?" He kept his gaze fixed on his hands. "What do you think?" He was the kindest natured, most easy-going person she knew. Could he really be contemplating killing someone?

He took a moment before answering. "I saw what he did to Eli." Jace looked up. His eyes were red-rimmed and raw. "He shot an unarmed, injured man in the head."

Caitlin gasped back a sob. She tried her best to focus but her mind wanted to conjure up images of what her husband's last moments would have been like. She was glad Micky stood his ground, still blocking her view of the front door. Nothing could block out the smell. A metallic odour, laced with something foul and sweet. She felt her stomach clench and another wave of nausea hit her, setting her teeth on edge.

"If you've both decided, why are you asking me?"

"We all have to be in agreement." His gaze was unflinching. "I'm talking about killing a man, there's no half measures. This will stick with you." He seemed about to say something but stopped.

"Do it." Once the words were out, she felt only relief. The humidity that had been hanging over the house all evening seemed to break and a cool breeze tumbled in from the kitchen, playing on her arms and shoulders.

Jace looked surprised. He'd been expecting her to argue with them, tell them how wrong it was to take a life whatever the circumstances. But she wasn't that person. That girl went into the cave and never came out.

"You sure?" Micky's voice was low, almost gentle.

Caitlin took a breath, careful to breathe through her mouth. "I wasn't much older than your sister when... A man did something. He killed my best friend. Hurt me in ways I can't..." She wanted them to understand. Not just for herself, but for Sharon. For Amy *and* for Eli. "After, when the police went to his house, he'd locked himself in the garage. He took his own life." She could see the shock on Jace's face. They'd known each other for years but she realised, no one had really known her since the day she came running out of the cave.

"There was no trial." She picked up the water bottle and took a sip. "I wouldn't let them examine me at the hospital. I was too... too broken." The water bottle shook in her hand so she set it back on the table. "Six weeks later, just after my fifteenth birthday, my mother took me to the doctor." She looked at Micky. His face was set, almost grim, dark green eyes holding hers. For some reason, what came next was easier to say while looking at him. "I was pregnant and the bastard who hurt me got away with it. I won't let it happen again."

"Cat, I didn't know. I–" Jace touched her hand and without thinking, she pulled away.

"No one knew. I never even told Eli." She looked at her hands, cut and bloodied. "I should have told him. Maybe things would have been different if I'd trusted him enough."

"He can't have gone far." Micky pulled her back into the moment. "No car. No shoes. There's a lot of blood, I'd say he's injured."

Jace stood. "Eli must have struggled with him before..." He hesitated. "Before, you know."

"No." Caitlin pulled the woollen blanket around her shoulders. "It was me. I stabbed him with a broken bottle."

Chapter Nineteen

Caitlin's story both shocked and sickened him. But, for such a small, fragile looking person, she had a lot of guts. The things that had happened to her, what she'd been through. Felix and the man who'd attacked Caitlin and her friend were like a plague, spreading their evil virus through despicable acts.

"You stabbed him?" He kept his tone level trying not to show how shocked he was by her admission. He noticed the way her hands shook, the haunted look in her eyes when she'd told her story. It had been tough to listen to, most likely torture for her to relive. He didn't want her to feel like he was judging her in any way.

She nodded and took another sip from the water bottle. "In the shoulder."

He could see by the look on her face, there was more to the story, but they needed to get going.

"Okay." He looked to Jace. "That gives us another advantage. The guy's a psychopath, but even psychos feel weak when they bleed."

Jace didn't answer. He sat with his hands dangling between his knees. Micky wondered if he was up to the work they had ahead of them. Finding Felix in the dark might be difficult. And then... would Jace have the stomach for what had to be done? Would *he*?

"Jace." He looked up, startled as if he had zoned out. "Are you sure you're up to this?" For a moment, Micky thought the kid would zone out again. *He's in shock.*

"Yeah, I'm up to it." Jace stood. "What now?"

"Now, we find him." He looked from Jace to Caitlin. "The gun he's carrying, there were five bullets in the clip. He's used three so, two left. Not much but enough. We need to be careful."

They both nodded. "We'll go out through the front and split up. I'll search the road and bushland at the front of the house." He turned to Jace. "You go around the back. Search the bush. Look for blood, footprints, and broken branches. Anything that tells us which way he's headed. After sixty minutes, we meet back here."

"Hang on." Caitlin stood, the blanket wrapped around her shoulders. He noticed her sway slightly to the right, steady herself, and straighten her spine. "What about me? I want to help."

Micky let out a long sigh. "You don't look so good." It was blunt but honest. Apart from the obvious injury to her ear and some cuts and scratches, he could see she was struggling. Her colour was off and her eyes looked glassy and feverish.

"He killed my husband. I'm not just going to sit here." She pulled the blanket tight around her body not quite meeting Micky's eyes. Since standing, her colour had gone from pale to almost grey.

"I don't have time to argue with you. You're not up to it, so you stay put."

She opened her mouth to argue, but then closed it again and sat down.

"There's a torch in the glove box. Jace, you should take it."

* * *

Before leaving, Micky turned on the outside lights, front and rear. It wasn't much but it would help give them an anchor point when it was time to return.

"Stay inside."

Caitlin held his gaze for a moment. Her eyes, like deep, rich moss regarded him with what he thought was worry. More churned behind those eyes than he could fathom. It made him uneasy. "We'll be back in an hour, one way or another."

They were standing near the sofas in the centre of the room, giving the body shrouded in yellow a wide birth.

"Be careful." Genuine concern edged her voice. She managed to look fragile and strong at the same time. He noticed a strand of reddish-gold hair plastered to her forehead and resisted the urge to brush it aside. Before he could answer, she'd turned to Jace. "You too. I can't lose anyone else. Understand?"

Jace moved to touch her but seemed to change his mind. Micky noticed the way the kid looked at his sister-in-law. He had feelings for her, it was almost painfully obvious, but he didn't think Caitlin noticed.

"Don't worry about me, Cat. I'm not easy to get rid of." He tried for a laugh, but to Micky's ears, it sounded forced, hollow.

"I know." Caitlin patted his arm, letting her hand linger for a second, closing her eyes as if whispering a silent prayer.

They filed outside in silence. Micky gave Jace his keys back so he could retrieve the torch from the car. In the few minutes it took him to open the vehicle and find the torch, Micky thought of lighting another cigarette. It had been years since he'd smoked, only taking the habit back up three days ago when he'd snatched Felix from outside the community swimming pool.

Absently, he fished the lighter and a squashed pack of smokes out of his back pocket. He stuck a cigarette in his mouth but didn't light it. Instead, let it dangle there for a moment. He had no doubts about what Felix had been up to at the swimming pool. Freaks like him were always hanging around places popular with kids. *I should have killed him that night.* If he'd had the guts to shoot Felix that first night, Eli would be alive and he wouldn't be dragging Jace into something that would weigh on his soul for the rest of his life. Micky pulled the unlit smoke from his mouth and crushed it.

"Okay. Ready." Jace turned on the torch. He was jittery. Micky could hear it in his voice, see the torchlight bouncing in his hands.

Micky held up the poker. He'd stashed it in the bushes near the front of the house when he'd taken it from Jace. "You'd better take this back. If you see him, don't take any chances. Put him out of action and tie him to a tree." He handed Jace a length of rope he retrieved from the back of his ute.

Jace seemed reluctant to take the weapon. Micky hoped the kid was going to be able to keep it together. *What am I doing? The guy isn't a killer. Neither am I.* But Felix was. Micky forced himself to picture his sister's face, as she was, the last time he'd seen her. It had been almost fifteen years, but he could remember her as clearly as if he'd spoken to her yesterday.

* * *

"Where are you off to?" He wiped grease on the front of his faded jeans and tossed the spanner onto an oily rag laid out on the lawn.

Amy bounced down the front steps, her shiny brown curls bobbing on her shoulders.

"I'm bored. I'm going to Melanie's house." She wore yellow shorts and a white top with frills around the cut-off sleeves. "She's got an instamatic camera, we're going to take photos and make an album."

"No." He reached into his back pocket and pulled out a packet of smokes. "I'm in the middle of changing the oil.

If you want a lift, you'll have to wait." He stuck a cigarette in his mouth. "Besides, Mum said you had homework."

"Done." Amy frowned. "I thought you were going to quit. Mrs Freemont, she teaches health, she said cigarettes give you lung cancer."

He couldn't help smiling. "Okay, okay. I'll quit, just not today." Micky lit the smoke. "Give me half an hour to finish and then I'll drop you at…um…"

"Melanie's." She finished for him. "It's okay, I want to catch the bus."

Micky let out a cloud of smoke. "No, Amy. I said I'd take you. You're too–"

"Please, Micky. I'm thirteen, not a baby. You can see the bus stop from here." She pointed across the road to a green bench with peeling paint. Micky noticed she was wearing a red-beaded friendship bracelet. "It's two stops to Melanie's house."

Micky scratched his chin. "Okay."

She let out a squeal and clapped her hands. "I love having you home."

He forced his face into what he hoped was a stern expression. "Don't get carried away. Write Melanie's address down next to the phone. I'll be there at…" He checked his watch. "At three o'clock to pick you up. That gives you three hours."

"Yes, sir." She gave him a mock salute then turned and scampered up the steps.

When Amy came back out, Micky was laying on his back, head under the old Ford Ranger. He heard the screen door clatter and shuffled his way out from under the bonnet. The sun, high in the cloudless sky blinded him for a second.

"Micky."

He threw an arm across his forehead to block out the glare. "Yeah?" Amy stood over him. For a second, the sun splayed out behind her making it seem like she had a silver-white halo. He felt the back of his neck stiffen and a cold finger of dread run down his spine.

"You okay, Micky?"

He pushed the feeling away and sprang to his feet. "Yeah, I'm fine. Just hungry," he lied. "Did you write down the girl's address?"

She rolled her eyes as if searching the heavens for help. It was a gesture so beyond her years that Micky couldn't help laughing.

"What's so funny?" She stuck her hand on her hip and stared at him with mock outrage. He could see a twinkle in her hazel eyes, it grew until she was laughing with him. "Seriously, Micky, you're as bad as Mum and Dad. They treat me like a baby. Don't you start."

He held up his hands. "Sorry. Sorry, I know you're not a baby anymore. What were you going to tell me?"

She made a clicking sound with her tongue and tilted her head to the side. In that instant, he could see her in ten years' time. Confident, but still sweet. Backpack slung over her shoulders heading off to trek through South America, a bespectacled boyfriend in tow. The idea pleased him and made his heart ache at the same time. Work took him away so much, she'd be grown and gone before he knew it.

"I made you something." Amy dug into the pocket of her shorts. "I was going to give it to you tonight, but Mum's planning one of her special dinners and… Well, I just want you to have it now." She held out her hand. A friendship bracelet like the one she wore but made with blue beads, the sun picked up the colour making the tiny stones glitter. "I know you can't wear it, but if you keep it in your pocket, it might–" She took a deep breath. "It might keep you safe."

"Thanks." He felt his throat tighten. *Must be going soft in my old age.*

He was twelve when his sister was born. A surprise baby was how his mother described her. But since the moment Micky laid eyes on her, he'd felt a connection to the kid. Not just because she was so much younger, although that was probably part of it. He'd never felt a moment's jealously or resentment towards his younger sibling, only a deep sense of pride and love.

"Okay. See you at three." Amy turned and headed down the faded red driveway, her sandals slapping the ground. When she got to the road, she made a big show of looking both ways before crossing.

He pulled another smoke out of the pack and lit up. She barely reached the bench when the green bus came chugging down the road. Just before it blocked her from view, she turned his way, smiled and raised her hand. He waved back, but the bus swept in front of her.

That was the last time he saw Amy. It was the last time anyone saw his little sister.

* * *

"Something wrong?" Jace's voice pulled him back to the moment with a start.

Micky flung the crushed cigarette into the bushes. "No. Just thinking about quitting smoking." He picked up another length of rope from near his feet. He checked his watch. "It's almost midnight. Be back here at 1:30 a.m. If we don't find him, we'll get in the vehicles and start searching. I'm pretty sure he headed west, but just to be sure he didn't go into the bush and double back, you check the back. He could be heading for the river."

Jace hesitated then said, "When we find him, who's… I mean which one of us is going to…" He let the question go unfinished.

"I'll do it." Micky jerked his chin towards the side of the house. "We need to get going. Felix won't hang around forever."

Chapter Twenty

The temperature dropped, bringing relief from the cloud of humidity that hung over the house like an ominous balloon. Caitlin felt the urge to pace. But every time she stood, the floor seemed to tilt and her stomach with it. In the end, she settled herself on the sofa and tried not to look at Eli's body.

Eli's body. When did her husband become a body? She shivered. Had the temperature really dropped or was the chill a symptom? Her leg throbbed. What started as a dull thumping now escalated into a boom. *Boom, boom,* keeping time with her heart. After years working as a doctor's receptionist, her medical knowledge was still limited to a half-remembered first aid course and what she read online. *Elevation,* the word popped into her head.

She swung her legs onto the sofa and risked a look at the bite. The two red bumps had transformed into purple lesions with angry lines of scarlet weaving up her calf. *I should have said something.* But telling Jace and Micky about the bite would have taken the decision out of their hands. They would have been left with no choice but to drive her to hospital and Felix… She couldn't stop seeing him: his mouth, lips swollen, tongue fleshy and pink, pressed to the gap in the cellar door. She couldn't stop hearing his sing-song voice, the vile things he had said. Whatever happened, Felix couldn't be allowed to get away with what he'd done.

It was a little after midnight. Micky and Jace had been gone less than ten minutes and the vastness of the house already worked on her nerves. The place felt too big, as if she were alone on an island. She needed to be doing something, anything to keep her mind off Eli laying near the front door.

Caitlin got up and started for the kitchen. Her leg felt heavy, weighted. She forced herself to keep moving, trying to ignore the painful bursts radiating up through her calf. She moved through the kitchen and opened the freezer side of the fridge. It had been turned off for a few hours, but still felt icy inside. She pulled out the cube tray and took it over to the sink.

After searching through the drawers below the island bench, she found a stack of clean tea towels. Taking a knife from the top drawer, she plunged the point into the cloths and split two of them down the middle. The third, she filled with ice cubes. Limping now, she took the shredded fabric and make-shift ice pack back to the sitting room.

Caitlin decided to at least try to stem the spread of spider venom. She tied the strips of fabric together to make one long length, then wrapped the length around her calf, taking care to cover the bite and secure the dressing as tightly as she could bare. When she'd finished, she pressed the ice-pack to the area of the bite.

It may have been her imagination, but the throbbing seemed to have receded. Caitlin lay her head on the arm of the sofa and stretched out. The idea of ten minute's sleep was tempting. She'd been running, fighting for her life. Now that it was over, her body craved rest. And more than just the physical exhaustion, telling her story to Jace and Micky left her feeling hollow—spent.

She checked her watch again. It was almost a quarter past midnight. The men would be back in just over forty-five minutes. There was nothing more she could do now so why not close her eyes? No sooner had she made the decision than her lids drifted down and Caitlin slept.

* * *

"You did it! You showed them what you could do." Her mother raised her glass, ice not so much clinked as crunched like bones breaking under foot.

Caitlin looked down and realised she was wearing her netball uniform. "Mum, why am I dressed like–"

"Don't worry about that now." Her mother waved a hand at her and bustled around the table.

They were in their old house on the outskirts of Mark Town in Queensland. Only her mother looked old. There were candles on the kitchen table. Caitlin couldn't remember ever seeing candles in their house because her mother was always afraid of starting a fire. *Good thing too. She's so drunk most nights, she'd burn the house down.* It was a nasty thing to think. Caitlin felt a rush of shame. Her mother drank a lot but loved her and tried to keep the house nice.

"Almost ready." Her mother's voice sounded strange, like she was half-singing. Caitlin didn't like it, she wished she could tell her to speak properly but the words didn't want to come out.

"Caitlin," her mother's shill voice pierced like a baby screaming. "I've made something special for you, for your birthday."

Caitlin's legs propelled her towards the table. The room was in darkness, the only light coming from the candles. There were so many, the flames melded together like bonfire. It wasn't right. None of it seemed normal. Caitlin didn't want to see what was on the table.

"That's it, love. It's all for you." Her mother leaned over the candles letting her greying hair dangle in the flames. *Why isn't her hair burning?* Her cheeks looked sunken, her eyes huge and shiny.

"What is it?" Caitlin barely recognised her own voice. It was as if a child spoke through her mouth. "Is it a birthday cake?"

Singing, faint but constant surrounded her. She reached the table. In the centre of the circle of candles sat a black bowl filled with golden balls, they glistened under the circle of flames. Each ball, no bigger than a grain of rice had a dot of black in the centre.

"Here." Her mother held out a spoon. "Eat them while they're warm."

Caitlin took the spoon, noticing the dirt under her mother's long yellowed fingernails. She didn't want to touch the golden balls. They reminded her of eyes, bird's eyes—beady and watchful. Like her legs, her hand moved of its own accord, plunging the spoon into the bowl and scooping the balls.

She didn't want to be in the house with her haggard-looking mother grinning at her like a Jolly Roger. But more than anything, she didn't want to eat the golden balls that looked like tiny eyes. Caitlin opened her mouth to protest and the spoon hit her tongue. It hit her tongue and lips again and again. Each time, dumping a spoonful of the strange balls into her mouth.

She held her breath, expecting the golden orbs to taste like poison, but instead they tingled on her tongue, oozing deliciousness. A combination of strawberry ice-cream and fairy-floss. She couldn't help herself, Caitlin gobbled the balls breathing in the sweet scent of spun sugar and strawberries.

The singing intensified until the room seemed to throb with the chant-like rhythm. A dart of agony cut through her middle and Caitlin doubled over.

"Mum, what's happening to me?" Caitlin clutched her belly, tears ran down her cheeks.

Her mother gave an enigmatic smile and tilted her pointy chin at the black bowl. Another stab pitched Caitlin forward. She opened her mouth to scream and a stream of vomit spewed out.

"They're alive." Her mother's voice rose to a shrill pitch.

Caitlin looked down at the contents of her stomach and felt like she was going mad. A mound of worms, long, thin and squirming lay at her feet. She could feel the creatures coating her teeth, hanging from her lips, alive and writhing. She looked up at her mother for help, but the woman had changed from a withered crone to a sharp featured scarecrow with burning eyes.

"No. No." Caitlin clamped her hands to her face and sprang forward. The sudden jolt brought her from nightmarish terror to stark reality. The sofa, dark and soft. The smell of leather and the brightness of the overhead lights.

She raised her head noticing the water bottle on the coffee table. Her brain struggled to make sense of her surroundings. Micky's house, the sitting room. *Eli.* It all came rushing back. As grim as the real world had become, it was better than the lingering memory of the dream.

Without thinking, she dragged the back of her hand across her mouth, half expecting to feel the squirming worm bodies dangling from her lips. She reached out a shaking hand and grabbed the water bottle. Desperate to rinse away the coated feeling from her tongue and teeth, she took a swig, letting the liquid swoosh around in her mouth before gulping it down. *Just a nightmare, that's all.* How could that be possible? She'd barely closed her eyes when the horrific reel began playing in her subconscious mind. It had to be another symptom brought on by the spider bite.

She looked at her watch, it was almost forty-five minutes since the men left. They'd be coming through the door any minute now. She raised herself up on her elbows wanting to see the open door, maybe spot Micky and Jace as they entered. Caitlin froze.

Something was wrong. The front door was shut. The door had been open when the men left, she was sure of it. Her scalp tingled as if pricked with a thousand tiny needles. She had the eerie sensation of being watched.

Her gaze fell on the yellow blanket. The form beneath it lay still. She let out a shaky sigh. Was it any wonder she felt spooked? Alone in the house with her husband's body. A night of violence and murder, who wouldn't let their imagination get the better of them? She turned away from the door and swung her feet off the sofa, tossing the ice-pack onto the coffee table.

A sound, so faint, she almost missed it. Like the rustle of fabric. No, more of a whisper than a real rustle. She snapped her head around and stared at the body under the blanket. Was she going insane or had the head moved?

Caitlin sat still, not allowing herself to blink. There was something off about Eli's body. It had changed in some way. Every nerve in her body quivered with the realisation—there was another presence in the room.

Chapter Twenty-one

With the wadded-up t-shirt pressed to his wound, Felix managed to stop the bleeding. He forced himself to take shallow breaths mostly through his nose. Over the years, he'd become a master at controlling his excitement. Not that they'd hear him, the three of them were really having a heart-to-heart. From his vantage spot, he could hear every word.

Kitty Cat started to speak. Her oh so sad voice grated on his nerves like squeaky wheels on a hospital trolley. She started talking about something that happened to her when she was a kid and his ears pricked up. *So, this wasn't her first rodeo, good for her.* He'd have liked to have known her back in the day. A mournful sigh almost slipped out, he caught himself just in time.

He listened carefully as Blyte explained the plan. He'd have bet his lunch money they were going to pile into the car and head for the nearest cop shop, but no. They had a *plan.* He forced his mind to slow and with it his heart rate. They really thought they could catch him like a desperate rat. It was almost too funny.

Things were working out even better than he'd hoped. All he had to do was wait—quietly. That, he could do.

Waiting was what he did best. Well, almost what he did best.

When this night was over, he'd walk away. No, he'd drive away. Dump the car somewhere and… his thoughts faltered. He couldn't go home again. There'd be doctors, questions, weekly urine tests. He'd be back to zombification. Besides, his blood was everywhere. At some point, someone would stumble upon the house and his DNA was on record. After this night, he'd move on. Start a new life. But for now, sit tight and breathe right.

Chapter Twenty-two

Swinging the torch in a tight arc, Micky followed the trail. Globs of blood, still damp, led from the front door, across the gravel driveway and into the bush. The trees were packed in clusters some more thinly spaced than others. Bordering the Myalup Forest, this was virgin bushland where tall stands of gum trees and ragged bushy natives crowded the terrain. Around him, the humming of insects mingled with the cries of owls and the occasional squawk of roosting native birds.

Less than fifteen metres into the bush, keeping track of the blood became almost impossible. Micky stopped moving and looked up at the sky. A blanket of darkness peppered with stars. The world seemed bigger at night, making finding Felix improbable. Micky had been in improbable situations in the past. He knew from experience sometimes the odds seem longer in the dark, but focus and persistence had a way of evening things up.

He pulled the end of his shirt out of his pants and wiped his face. The temperature had dropped, but he could still feel the heat of the day leaching out of the ground, rising like steam off a hot pan. Micky moved deeper into the bush, eyes focused for signs of disruption. Something about the trail didn't sit right.

Pausing, he recounted his movements. He'd followed the blood from where it left the gravel and entered the bush. Apart from a few splatters on low-lying branches, he'd seen no other traces to indicate Felix came this way. But that couldn't be right. He swore softly and stopped moving. Time to double back and sweep to the right.

Ten minutes later he was back to the split in the bush where he began. It would be pointless going left. That way would ultimately lead to the back of the house, an area already covered by Jace. Micky swivelled his head in that direction. The lights from the second story were the only sign of life in the moonless night. Distant and golden light from a place where nothing good happened. Caitlin was there, waiting. Coming back empty-handed would be letting her *and* Amy down.

He turned from the house and plunged back into the trees, this time veering sharply to the right. Under the artificial light of the torch, the bush turned silver. A few metres ahead, something moved. A crackle of dry leaves and twigs betraying the position. Micky clicked off the torch and froze. He could smell eucalyptus mixed with rot, the odours of the forest. No trace of human sweat or blood in the air.

Something heavy thudded through the trees. Micky took a step in the blackness and let the shotgun slip off his shoulder. Inching closer with the gun at his side, he listened. Another thump and something broke through the trees. He clicked on the torch, the light shining into the large glassy eyes of a kangaroo. The animal froze as if expecting a bullet.

Micky relaxed his grip on the shotgun. As if sensing the danger had passed, the roo ducked its head and came up chewing. It was small with slim shoulders. Too big to be a wallaby, clearly a doe. Micky side-stepped to give the creature her space, but his forward movement spooked the grazing animal and with lightning speed she bounced into the cover of the bushes. The creature disappeared as if swallowed by the dense growth.

He shone the light on his watch. It had been thirty minutes since Jace headed for the rear of the house. Maybe Felix *had* doubled back. There was every chance he'd headed for the river. Even though he was pretty sure there *was* no trail to find, Micky tossed up the idea of veering further right, searching for twenty minutes or back-tracking in case he missed something. He turned off the torch and stood in the dark. Since returning to the house and finding it hijacked by Jace and his family, Micky's brain had been in overdrive. What he needed was to clear his mind and listen to his gut.

As always, in quiet moments, Amy invaded his thoughts. Her voice as she walked down the driveway towards the road. Her arm raised, a carefree wave. The images were so familiar, like an old photograph worn and aged from years of handling. The frozen picture, faded. He forced his sister out of his mind and found silence.

The hush turned into another voice. Soft, with an undercurrent of melancholy, he heard Caitlin. *I stabbed him with a broken bottle.* Blood on the gravel, almost black in the white light from the torch. Large drops. *Too large.*

He clicked the switch, illuminating the area around him. If Felix had been trying to escape, the bloody trail would have been thinner. Smaller drops as he hurried away from the house. Maybe even a narrow line of blood. It had bothered Micky since they left the house. The bloody trail was too easy to spot *and* follow. *The large drops...* it was as if Felix paused giving the blood time to drip.

He turned back searching for the upstairs lights. For a moment, he saw only darkness. It was as if he'd walked off the edge of the world and could find no point of reference. His chest tightened. He turned in a circle, his movements jerky and clumsy. In his panic, he almost missed the light. So distant, the golden glow almost didn't register.

He ran, the torch's beam bouncing around, bathing the bush in a wintery-blue that seemed desolate and endless. *A place where nothing good happens.* Why did he leave her alone? It was a stupid mistake, one he hoped Caitlin wouldn't pay for.

Chapter Twenty-three

The feet. Why hadn't she noticed earlier? Or maybe there'd been nothing to notice. Caitlin inched to the edge of the sofa, wincing as the leather squeaked beneath her thighs. She'd been asleep for at least half an hour. Long enough for someone to tamper with her husband's body?

The nightmare had left her shaken. More than shaken—completely rattled. *I'm awake now and I know those aren't Eli's feet.* She swallowed and stood. Two years ago, Eli was standing on a glass outdoor table trying to sweep cobwebs from the ceiling of their tiny gazebo. Caitlin recalled the old familiar feeling of irritation. A few stray fibres in the corners, barely noticeable unless you were Eli. Still, he wouldn't be dissuaded. Balancing on the table, one foot on the metal rim, the other on the glass, he set about cleaning the ceiling with an upturned broom. The table collapsed under him, aged and brittle glass shattering into thousands of razor sharp shards. He was lucky, eighteen stitches across the sole of his right foot and one night in hospital.

Standing beside the sofa, Caitlin could see the bare feet peeking out from under the yellow blanket. Similar to Eli's in size, but minus the long, jagged scar. The pool of congealed blood on the left of the body was as she remembered: a two-metre-wide puddle with wads of sodden tea towel plonked amidst the liquid like dark clots. Just looking at the mess made her stomach churn.

Caitlin glanced to the right and noticed a smear of blood on the greyish brown stone flooring. Almost a skid. The details registered in the blink of an eye. Together with the missing scar, she had no doubt the body was not Eli.

A breeze from somewhere behind her, most likely the back door, fluttered across her spine like cool fingers. She shuddered and took a step backwards. If it wasn't Eli, then it had to be Felix.

As if thinking the man's name evoked the rising of the dead, the body moved, head turning from angled right to straight ahead. Caitlin almost believed she was still in the midst of the nightmare. However, the cold stone under her feet felt all too real. She should have been running, screaming for help, but instead she stayed rooted to the spot. Watching, mouth agape, as the corpse sat up and pulled the yellow rug away from its face.

"Made you look." Felix gave a snort.

Caitlin hesitated, still trying to process what was happening. In the blink of an eye, he was on his feet and moving towards her. The gun was stuffed, barrel first, into the waistband of his pants. The bruising on his face glowed under the lights giving his skin the appearance of a ripe plum.

"I don't want to shoot you." His tone was calm, conversational. "All this." He waved an arm towards the stairs. "It's Blyte's doing. Not mine."

Her mind raced, weighing up the chances of making it through to the kitchen and out the back door before Felix could pull the gun and shoot her. Jolts of pain, like tiny electrical shocks, cut through her calf. Even if both her legs were working, she doubted she could make it out of the house before taking a bullet in the back.

"You didn't have to shoot my husband." She hoped stalling him would give Micky and Jace time to get back to the house.

"He was going to drive away and leave me here." Felix's voice rose slightly. He was almost at the edge of the sofa now. "I couldn't just let him get away with that." The blood on the left side of his shirt caught her gaze. With one eye swollen almost shut, it was difficult to read his expression. "I'm not a bad person." He shuffled forward. "I'm the victim here." He pointed at the front door. "I was telling the truth about Blyte abducting me and locking me in the cellar. All you had to do was drive me to the hospital."

"Why don't you just go? There's nothing stopping you leaving." She tried to keep her voice even as if they were old friends discussing a problem.

"With no car keys?" He held his hands up in a gesture of helplessness and winced. "No. I'll wait. When they get back, I'll shoot them." His mouth slackened as though he were caught in a daydream. "I have no choice, he'd never let me go."

"You mean Micky?" She shuffled back a few centimetres hoping he wouldn't notice. She tried to think of a way out so that when Jace and Micky came through the door, they'd stand a chance.

"Micky?" He cocked his head to the side. "Your old man's barely room temperature and you're already getting friendly with the next thing that comes your way?" There was an edge to his voice now, cruelty bordering on anger. "I think Eli was right when he called you a slut."

She kept her expression bland. "You've got the gun, he can't stop you. No one else needs to get hurt."

"I heard your story." He continued as if she hadn't spoken. "I wish I'd met fourteen-year-old Caitlin." A smile lifted one side of his mouth. "But from what you said, someone beat me to it." There was a light in his shifting brown eyes. Caitlin realised he wasn't only a sexual predator, Felix enjoyed inflicting pain too.

She felt a flicker of anger. Men like Felix and Campson, they didn't just want to use young girls. It wasn't enough to invade their bodies, they wanted to destroy them, body and soul. Torture them in any and all ways possible. She looked down so he wouldn't see the disgust in her eyes. *If I had a weapon, I'd kill him myself.* With the thought came an idea. She'd left a knife on the counter when she cut up the tea towels. If she could get him into the other room, she might stand a chance.

"His name was Campson. Andrew Campson." It hurt just to say his name, but she made herself keep talking. Felix enjoyed pain, she bet he'd be hungry for gory details.

His mouth, swollen and cut, dropped open slightly like a salivating pig. She felt a mixture of satisfaction and repulsion. She had his attention, now all she had to do was get him into the kitchen.

"He offered us a ride, my friend Sharon and I." The tremor in her voice wasn't forced. "We had no reason *not* to trust him. He worked at the Civic Centre where we played netball. I'd seen him around town." She covered her face with her hands and turned away stumbling a few steps closer to the kitchen. She could hear Felix's breathing, heavy and excited.

"Was he rough with you?" The question took her by surprise. There was a gentle quality to his voice. She could imagine that tone worked well on children.

"I can't." She took another step. "I don't know why I'm telling you these things." Another step. "I need a drink. A real drink." She took her hands away from her face. "Do you mind?"

The steeliness in his gaze caught her off guard. She let out a gasp and quickly sniffed, hoping it sounded more like a sob. He didn't answer at first, just held her with his unwavering stare. It was as if he were looking for something, searching her face and voice for deception.

"Why not." That gentle tone again. If she didn't know better, she'd believe he actually cared.

Walking towards the kitchen, Caitlin had to suppress the urge to run. She could feel Felix's eyes on her, sliding over her body like the writhing worms in her nightmare. She wondered if him letting her enter the kitchen might be a trick. A way of making her turn her back so he could shoot her. No, she'd seen it in his eyes, Felix would want her looking at him when he killed her.

Her right leg felt stiff as if the knee were heavy with fluid. She took deliberate steps, not letting him know she was limping. The worst thing she could do would be to let a predator like Felix see any signs of weakness.

"Okay, Kitty Cat. Stop there." He spoke from behind her. They were in the kitchen, just past the archway. "Don't think I've forgotten what you did to me in the cellar." He touched her shoulder. His fingers were dry and cold yet she felt her skin burn with revulsion under his touch. "I'm only giving you this one warning. Try anything and I won't waste a bullet on you." His breath blew past her ear. "I'll use my hands."

She had the feeling he was waiting for her to answer. "Okay." He let go of her shoulder. Her hand itched with the need to rub the spot where he'd touched her.

She pressed her lips together and walked towards the fridge. Out of the corner of her eye, she could see the knife on the island bench. She wondered if he'd noticed it too.

"I'm starting to think I should take you with me. I think we have a connection, you and me."

The back door was open, cool night air wafted through the opening. There was a glimpse of black and the sound of frogs as she opened the fridge. The sight and smell of the world outside the house made her want to weep. Eli would never see the sky again. For him, the sun had set for the final time. Not because of a long illness or an accident while doing something he loved, but on the whim of a sadist. Caitlin's hand closed around a can of beer.

"Do you want one?" She spoke over her shoulder.

"I don't drink." He sounded prissy, as if the thought of alcohol offended him. "You never answered my question."

Caitlin moved around the island bench and began opening cupboards, playing for time while inching her way towards the knife.

The sound of his palm slapping the benchtop made her jump. "Stop doing that." The gentle coxing tone vanished, replaced by rage.

She froze, the beer held to her chest. The suddenness of his anger threw her off balance. His moods shifted so violently, he seemed off-balance. She felt tears stinging her eyes and with the tears came exhaustion. "I'm sorry." It was all she could manage.

"Answer my question." Felix placed both hands on the island bench, palms down. "Was he rough with you?" He spoke slowly, enunciating every word.

She was running out of time. Jace and Micky would be back at any second. And when they arrived, they'd be walking into a trap. Felix would shoot them. Unless, she could find a way of stopping him.

"Yes." Her voice was little more than a whisper. "He… he was rough."

Felix sniffed and tilted his head back as if her words were scented with the pain and abuse she'd suffered. With his gaze off her, Caitlin moved to the left. The knife was within reach. She held the can in her right hand so that meant picking up the knife with her left.

He dropped his head. "You mentioned your friend." He drummed his fingers on the benchtop. "How did he kill her?"

She forced herself to meet his gaze. "He strangled her." It was the first time she'd repeated that part of the story in fifteen years. The day it happened, she recounted the details to a female police officer, her mother by her side. They'd tried to make her go to the hospital, but she refused.

"I just want to say it. What he did, and go home."

The police woman nodded and turned on a tape recorder. Caitlin thought it looked old-fashioned. It was a stupid thing to be thinking about when she had just left her best friend to be murdered.

"Oh Caitlin." His voice snapped her out of the memory. "And you so young." There it was, that gentle tone. To an outsider, someone who hadn't seen Felix shoot Eli in cold blood and then rampage through the house like a lunatic, he would sound genuinely moved.

He closed his eyes, frowning as if thinking about what she'd said caused him pain. She couldn't hesitate, it might be her only chance. Her arms felt wooden and her throat tight. She reached out, fingers splayed. The knife only centimetres from her grasp when Felix's hand snatched the weapon up.

He made a clicking sound with his tongue. "I did warn you." He waved the blade back and forth in front of his face. "It's like you're stupid." His voice rose, "What do I have to do to make you understand?"

"I'm sorry, I–"

"No. I don't know what it is about you, Kitty Cat." He waved the knife in a circle. "I should just get rid of you now, but instead I'm going to do you a favour." He flashed a sad smile. "I told you, I'm not a bad person, just… different."

She glanced over her shoulder wishing she'd made a run for it when she was near the back door. All she'd done was make things worse. Now he had the gun and the knife.

"Give me your hand." He reached out to her.

"What?" They were on opposite sides of the bench. "Why?"

Felix reached across and grabbed her wrist. She tried to pull away but his fingers clamped on like a manacle. He squeezed and she felt the bones in her wrist grinding.

"Stop, or I'll break it." He gave her wrist a sharp twist.

It felt like her hand wrenched free of her arm: tendon, muscle and bone stretching. The pain flared upwards making her cry out. She had no choice but to stop fighting his grip. Caitlin let her hand go limp in his grasp and in return, he stopped twisting.

"That's it." He turned her hand over and placed it on the bench, palm down. "Here's the part where I do something nice for you."

His fingers held her hand against the benchtop. The pain in her wrist lessened but still burned. He was saying something. She tried to force her mind to focus, but the pain made it hard to concentrate.

"I'm going to let you save one of them."

That got her attention. She looked up. Her hair had fallen across her face, stringy and damp with sweat and blood. It obscured her vision, but she could make out his eyes. They were muddy, flat and alert at the same time. It made her think of the way wild animals watch their prey.

"What are you talking about?" she asked. The breeze must have dropped because there didn't seem to be enough air in the room.

"When they get back, I'm going to shoot them, take the keys and go." He held the knife up in front of his face. "Now this is the interesting part. Because you've sort of grown on me, I'll shoot one of them in the leg. The other... Well, he'll be the unlucky one."

She couldn't believe what he was saying. He wanted her to choose who lived and who died. It was unthinkable. "I don't believe you." She tried to jerk her wrist away, but his grip was too strong. "This is just another game. A way of torturing me."

"I like games, Kitty Cat." His swollen eye twinkled under the kitchen lights. "It's all a game, haven't you realised that by now?" He made a clicking sound with his tongue. "You're too old for my usual games, but I think this could be fun."

She was crying now. The tears ran down her cheeks and dripped off her chin. The can slid out of her free hand and hit the stone with a wet thud. Beer hissed across the floor coating her feet.

Felix shook his head. "Make a choice. We both know they'll be back soon. Isn't that why you tried to distract me with the grisly details of your molestation?" His voice was reprimanding, but calm. "I'll count to three. One."

He used his thumb to spread her fingers so that her pinkie was splayed. Holding the knife at a sharp angle, he put the point between her pinkie and ring finger.

Caitlin's heart thudded in her throat. "Please. Felix, don't." Even as she begged, part of her could see it was useless.

"Two." His grip was on the handle of the knife, poised to cleave downwards.

Tiny details registered with magnified clarity. The twin spots of white foam at the corners of his mouth. The open pores on her tormentor's nose.

"Who's going to be the lucky man?"

She tried curling her fingers back but the pressure of his hand on hers allowed for no movement. The blade pressed on the flesh just below the knuckle.

"No. Please," she heard the terrified pleading and barely recognised it as her own voice.

"Three."

He raised his shoulder as if doing some sort of half-shrug. When the blade came down, she heard a crack, felt a pop. There was no pain and then her nerves reacted. Caitlin's head snapped back hard enough to clang her teeth together. A scream started in her chest and built until it released like a storm siren. Her legs buckled but didn't quite give out.

He must have put the knife down because his hand closed around her right forearm lending support and balance. She could hear him speaking, but not the actual words. Her body shuddered.

"Caitlin." He pulled her closer, their faces only centimetres apart. "Micky or Jace? Who lives?"

Her hand felt warm, wet. She didn't want to look at the benchtop. Couldn't bear to see what she knew would be lying there amidst the blood. And all the while, Felix kept talking. Even through blurred vision, she could see the knife. It gleamed under the kitchen light.

Something touched her finger. A jolt of agony took her breath away. Cold steel against her ring finger.

"I'm going to count to three. Make a choice, because I can do this nine more times." Somehow, his words broke through the pain and shock.

"Stop." She batted the hand gripping her wrist. "Don't. Felix, stop." The pain was unbearable, but the prospect of going through another assault on her hand was worse than the way the air felt against her exposed bone. "You don't have to be a monster." Her voice was a hiccupping whisper. "You can stop... stop hurting people."

His blinked as if a series of flashes were exploding in front of his eyes. When he focused on her again, there were tears, shiny and unshed on his lower lids. "I do have to be a monster, at least to people like Blyte and your brother-in-law."

"No, you–"

"One." There had been a glimpse of something, maybe regret. For an instant, she'd thought she'd reached him; heard real emotion in his voice, but whatever ugly compulsion controlled him was too strong.

"I'm begging you, don't."

"Two... Who lives, Caitlin?"

She could see his shoulder rising in that same half-shrug. Her mouth opened trying to speak, but the words stuck in her throat.

"Thr—"

"Micky." It came out around a sob. "Micky. Micky."

He released her wrist and withdrew the knife. "It didn't have to be that difficult."

The room tilted. She tried to stop herself from falling by grabbing the bench with her uninjured hand. A few seconds of dimness and blessed silence and then the kitchen came back into focus. Felix had his back to her. He tossed something aside. The hush was fractured with a metallic clang as the knife landed on the stone floor. Caitlin moved her left hand slowly, cradling it to her chest.

"Caitlin?" Someone called her name.

Chapter Twenty-four

Following the erratic jumping arc of the torch, Micky ran through the bush towards the house. The upstairs lights made the building look more like a ghost ship sailing through the night than a house. Around him, dense bush tore at his clothes, barring his path. He was moving too fast, not taking time to watch his footing. Something whipped the side of his face, almost catching the corner of his eye.

How could he have been so stupid? Why didn't he think to search the house before leaving her alone? The answer was simple. His obsession with Felix overrode his judgement. It clouded every aspect of his life, had done for years. Even the house itself was nothing more than a stage, constructed so he could play out his desire for revenge. Built to his specifications, designed to be impenetrable and unescapable. But it all backfired on him. One man was dead and Caitlin... He couldn't bear to think what might be happening to her.

The light landed on a crop of trees, tightly packed and surrounded by a thick tangle of vines. Micky cursed and slowed down. He dropped his hands onto his knees and sucked in a few breaths. Going around would add precious minutes to his journey, but he had no choice.

Cutting right, he skirted a solid mass of trees and foliage until the area opened up enough for him to slip through the shrubs and pick up the pace. He was getting closer. The outside lights came into view. He could hear his own breathing, sharp and rapid, competing with the sound of his boots thumping the ground.

Micky felt the trees thinning and stepped up his speed. His left foot came down on something hard that rolled under the sole of his boot. A sudden view of the sky and he was on his back, shotgun biting into his shoulder. The torch bounced away under a lacy-looking bush. He lay motionless hoping to give his heart time to return to somewhere near normal before pushing on.

A scream cut through the darkness, sudden and jagged with pain. Micky felt cold sweat break out on his body, chilling him to the bone. He rolled sideways and snatched the torch from its hiding place under the bush. In a fluid forward motion, he was on his feet and running. This time, his feet skimmed the ground. He wasn't sure how he managed to keep his footing only that somehow, in the tangle of grass and shrubs, he found his way.

It wasn't until Micky crunched down on the driveway that he almost lost his footing a second time. His boots skidded, a shower of stones sprayed the side of Eli's car. Micky's palm slapped the bonnet of the dark-coloured compact vehicle, a fraction of a second before his hip made contact with it. Momentum carried him forward, almost spilling him over the bonnet. The lightweight aluminium groaned under his weight, then dipped.

Not bothering to stop and check the damage to the car or his hip, Micky bolted for the front door. He pulled up just short of the entrance only to find it closed. It was open when they left, that was clear in his mind. He tried the door, relieved to find it unlocked. Not sure what might be waiting on the other side, he opened the heavy slab as silently as possible.

The house reeked of death. It occurred to him how quickly a human being went from a vital presence to something offensive to the senses. An affront to the living.

In spite of the smell, there was no sign of Eli's body. The area just beyond the Blackwood sideboard was bare save a pool of blood and the yellow blanket. Micky scanned the sitting room but could see no sign of a struggle.

"Caitlin?" Announcing his presence was risky, but if she was hiding, he wanted her to know he was there. Besides, Felix knew Micky would be back, why else would he have hung around?

Micky slid the shotgun off his shoulder and edged his way along the wall leading to the study. He scanned the room a second time and noticed a tea towel on the coffee table sitting in a puddle of water. The dark wool blanket Caitlin had wrapped around her shoulders lay in a pile on the sofa.

He was starting to get a picture of what must have happened while he was gone. Caitlin on the sofa, maybe asleep. Felix hiding somewhere, waiting like a cunning little shithouse rat. When the coast is clear he ambushes her. It wasn't a pretty picture. Less than ten minutes had passed since he heard her scream, he hoped he wasn't too late.

The study door stood open. He stopped and listened. A sound came from the direction of the kitchen—an echoing sob. A desperate noise that made his skin prickle. It had to be Caitlin. Torn between checking the study and heading straight for the kitchen, Micky hesitated. The smart move would be checking all the rooms on the ground floor. *I should have checked before leaving her alone.*

Another sound, this one weaker: a whisper. Micky made up his mind and moved past the study. He brought the shotgun up and clicked off the trigger guard. Felix was armed, with two bullets left in the clip. Entering the kitchen would make Micky an easy target. He weighed his options but could see no alternative. Going around to the back door would waste time and he didn't know if Felix had locked it. His only chance was distracting Felix and hoping he'd be slow to react.

* * *

Caitlin heard Micky's voice. He called her name and then silence. She was still on the far side of the bench opposite Felix. He faced the archway, his back to her. *He said he wouldn't kill him.* But Felix was a psychopath, capable of anything.

His arm was moving, even from behind she knew he was pulling the gun out of his waistband. A feeling of mistiness clouded her mind making it difficult to think. Colours played around the edges of her vision.

"Don't hurt him. You said you wouldn't kill him," she whispered or maybe the words were in her head. *I should be screaming, warning him.* "Felix, you promised you wouldn't kill him."

If Felix heard her, he gave no indication. His arm was raised now, pointing the gun at the archway. She looked down at the benchtop. Through tangled hair and blurred vision, she saw blood. The marble top was awash in her blood, bright and fresh. So red it seemed unreal. Her finger, the nail painted with clear polish, lay amidst the mess. She gagged and slumped against the counter still clutching her left arm.

She opened her mouth to call out, warn Micky but his name was a croak, barely audible. Something moved behind her, scraping. She was losing focus. The mistiness clouding her thoughts, pulled at her like ghostly hands trying to drag her underwater.

Resisting the pull, Caitlin used her uninjured hand to grasp the benchtop. Holding something solid helped bring her vision into focus. She lifted her left leg and slid her knee onto the marble top. She felt her leg slide through liquid. An image tried to manifest in her mind but she pushed it away and climbed sideways like a crab, flopping her stomach onto the bench.

Something flew through the archway. A blur of grey. She was on the island bench now, kneeling behind Felix. From her vantage spot, she could see his arm, rigid and locked at the elbow. Fleetingly, it occurred to her that after everything he'd done, his hand wasn't even shaking. Felix's head moved along with his arm, tracking whatever flew through the door.

Caitlin dipped her head and spoke into his ear, "Felix."

As he turned, she wrapped her left arm around his neck, hardly feeling the drilling pain in her hand. With her uninjured hand, she grabbed the arm holding the gun. The moment she touched him, Felix leapt forward, taking Caitlin with him. Her bloody hand slipped, almost losing traction on his neck. Her fingers found his shoulder wound, the one she'd inflicted, and grasp the fleshy depression.

The gun blasted, something split with a wooden crack. Felix clawed at her hand, gouging her severed finger. Caitlin howled like an injured dog and felt herself sliding downwards.

"Let go! Let go!" Shouts, barely audible over the ringing in her ears. Blinded by pain to the point of losing all sense of understanding, Caitlin hung on.

Felix swung right and Caitlin felt a second of lightness then impact, hard enough to knock the air out of her lungs. Another shot rang out, the burst of sound impossibly loud in the confines of the kitchen. She opened her mouth, desperate for air and sucked in the sickening odour of chemicals and wet sawdust.

Turmoil raged around her. Shouts, crashing, and all the while a ringing in her ears. She tried to open her eyes and lift her head, but bile filled her mouth. Caitlin managed to turn her face to the side and let the foul-tasting liquid spill out. Her eyelids closed and the cacophony fell into silence.

* * *

Micky spotted the candlestick. For some reason, it had been placed on a kitchen stool just below one of the front windows. He crossed the room and took hold of the heavy ornament. He needed something, anything to distract Felix long enough for him to enter the kitchen and get the man in his sights. The sitting room offered slim pickings. The emptiness of the house hadn't struck him until now. *It was never meant to be a home.*

With no time to waste, he skirted the walls and made his way towards the archway leading to the kitchen. More whispering, too faint to make out words, but clearly Caitlin's voice. He moved towards the sound, grateful for the noise that was blocking out the sound of his boots on the stone.

At the edge of the kitchen entrance, he paused. The whispering ceased. The only sound came from his own heartbeat racing in his ears. He stepped away from the wall and positioned himself on an angle. A wedge of floor and cabinet became visible, but no sign of Felix. *He'll be at the bench.* It was the obvious place to wait. Centre of the room, good view of the archway. In Felix's place, Micky would have gone with the wall on the other side of the entrance, but Felix was a civilian, untrained in combat. He knew how to stalk a victim, but only a helpless one.

With the candlestick raised, ready to toss, he hesitated. For an instant, he thought he heard his name, but the sound was covered by another noise, wood on stone. The back door opening. Either Jace was coming in or Felix was trying to get out. Either way, there was no more time for hesitation.

Micky tossed the candlestick at an angle which would see it hit the kitchen floor just to the left of the archway. The ornament crashed into the stone with a metallic twang. Micky burst into the kitchen, shotgun raised.

He wasn't sure what he'd been expecting. His mind had blanked out the possibilities—the things Felix might have done to Caitlin. What he wasn't prepared for was Felix turning madly, covered in blood with Caitlin clinging to his back.

He brought the shotgun to his shoulder. "Let go!" He couldn't get a clear shot at Felix for fear of hitting Caitlin.

The gun wavered up and then down. Instinctively Micky ducked. A bullet zinged past his shoulder and clipped the cabinets on the left of the archway. The wood splintered and cracked like a walnut.

"Let go!" he tried one more time to get Caitlin's attention before giving up and tossing the shotgun back into the sitting room. If he was going to disarm Felix, he'd have to use his hands.

No sooner had Micky dropped his weapon than Felix spun Caitlin to the right, sending her sailing through the air and crashing into the cellar door. Before Felix could turn and raise the gun, Micky charged. He rammed his shoulder into Felix's chest and drove him back across the island bench. As his back hit the marble, an *oomph* of shocked air burst out of Felix's mouth.

Micky grabbed for the gun, tipping Felix backwards until he was laying on the benchtop with Micky on top of him. Felix was smaller and injured, but he held fast to the gun, squirming and shifting under Micky's weight.

"Give it up." Their faces were close enough for Micky to feel Felix's breath on his cheek. He could see the man's eyes shifting with a mixture of viciousness and panic, the whites rolling into view like a shark about to strike.

Micky jammed his left forearm into Felix's throat and pressed. A foam of spittle hit Micky, landing just above his mouth. With his right hand, he grappled for the gun, Felix holding it over the edge of the counter, just beyond Micky's reach. He could see Felix's finger on the trigger. Everything else seemed to narrow until all Micky could see was the muzzle, black and gaping as it turned towards him.

He tried to throw himself forward so his hand would jar Felix's grip and knock the muzzle away from its trajectory. Even as he shoved off the floor, Micky knew he would be too late. The muzzle, cocked at an awkward angle in Felix's hand, trained on Micky's face.

In a fraction of a second, fifteen years of grief and anger seemed to shrivel and die under the pointlessness of what was about to happen. There was no rage left in Micky, only regret. He felt a cool wind brush his face. There was time to wonder if it were some kind of backdraft signalling a bullet to the brain. Then a slingshot of blurred movement. A thud, then a blast of sound turned the world into a chamber of echoes.

Micky let out a cough of breath and blinked. He let go of Felix and pushed back, unsure if he were hit or not. The gun slid out of Felix's hand. If it made a noise when it hit the floor, Micky couldn't tell. It felt like his ears were filled with gum. Felix's body, now free of Micky's weight slid off the bench and slumped to the floor almost knocking Micky's legs out from under him.

Micky shook his head, trying to dislodge the ringing from inside his ears. It was only then he saw Jace and the last few seconds snapped together. Standing on the other side of the bench, Jace held the candlestick.

Micky looked from Jace down to Felix. The right side of his forehead, just above the temple, was dented; his skull had collapsed in on itself. A trickle of dark, oily blood ran out of his ear.

"You stopped him from shooting me?" Micky's mouth worked and a garbled series of noises bubbled in his ears. He hoped his words sounded a bit clearer to the other man.

Jace's mouth moved. Micky pointed to his ear and shook his head. Nodding his understanding, Jace set the candlestick down on the bench amidst a network of bloody swirls. Micky spotted the gun on the floor and stepped forward kicking it away from Felix's hand. The gun was empty and Felix was in no condition to try anything, still Micky felt relieved when the weapon was out of reach.

Micky turned, searching for Caitlin. The last time he'd seen her she was airborne, hitting the cellar door and crumpling to the floor. To his relief, she was already struggling into a sitting position.

Crossing the room, he felt a whooshing pop in his ears, similar to the sensation he'd experienced in an aeroplane. Sound came crashing back: Jace's voice, frogs in the distance, and Caitlin saying his name.

"Micky. I thought he shot you." She sounded sleepy as if ready for a long overdue nap.

"So did I." He crouched down in front of her. "We need to get you to a hospital."

Her hand was bleeding heavily, she held it cradled against her chest. "What about him?" She jerked her chin towards Felix. Her head bobbed as if keeping it from sinking onto her chest was taking a great effort.

"We've wasted enough time on him."

He thought he saw the ghost of a smile touch the edges of her mouth. It appeared and vanished so quickly it might have been a trick of the light.

"He's alive," Jace spoke from the other side of the room. "He's got a pulse. I'm going to tie him up before we go."

Micky reached out and brushed a strand of hair from Caitlin's cheek. Her fingers brushed his and for a second, he couldn't speak. "Sit tight." Her head moved again, almost a nod. There were still a few things to take care of before they left.

Micky wrapped a towel around Caitlin's hand while Jace stowed the shotgun under the false shelf. He wanted to ask about her finger, but judging by the look in her eyes when he wrapped her wound, he decided to let it go for now. It was clear Felix had tortured her, cutting off her finger for God knows what reason. Pushing her for answers now would only make things worse.

Jace handed him the gun. "What about this? We can't hide this from the cops—Not with Eli…"

Micky flicked the release and ejected the clip. He bent over Felix's unconscious form. His chest rose and fell in a steady motion. It occurred to Micky that he could finish all this in less than a minute. Felix was unconscious, maybe even dying, there'd be no resistance. He went as far as resting his hand on Felix's chest. Would it make any of their lives easier? He'd wasted so many years of his life brooding about Felix Holly and what he'd done to Micky and his family, he wouldn't give him this too. Not a moment's guilt, better to let the cops deal with him. Micky thought of Jace whispering to his dead brother. Micky had enough regrets without adding Felix's life to the list.

There would be prints on the clip, Micky used his shirt to wipe them away and then rolled Felix onto his stomach so he could reach the man's hands, bound behind his back. Micky pressed Felix's limp fingers to the empty magazine. Then using his shirt to hold the clip, he inserted it back into the gun.

"It'll be light soon." Jace stood by the back door. He sounded older than he had a few hours ago. Outside, the darkness thinned to a watery grey.

Micky dropped the gun on the counter. He walked over to Caitlin. For an instant, he thought she might have stopped breathing. His heat jumped, pounding against his ribs. Her eyelids opened, a glimpse of green.

"I'm holding tight." The strength in her voice surprised him.

Micky slipped his arm around her back. "Time to go." He helped her to stand.

As they left the kitchen, he noticed her eyes never wavered towards Felix. It was as if, for her, he no longer existed. *If she can do it, so can I.*

The three of them walked through the sitting room. Jace reached the front door first and stopped. He turned to Micky, his eyes shiny with unshed tears.

Micky saved Jace from having to ask. "I think he's in the study."

Jace opened his mouth to speak, cleared his throat and tried again. "He moved him?" There was pain in his voice, fresh and raw. Micky had seen the same look he'd seen in the mirror countless times over the years. When the pain became familiar, it morphed into bitterness and soured every moment—if you let it.

Jace turned towards the study, but Caitlin reached out her hand to him. She touched his arm as she'd done earlier in the evening. "Don't look, Jace. Please don't."

His cheeks coloured and Micky could see the muscles in his jaw bunching as if he wanted to shake her hand off. Instead, his shoulders slumped and he patted Caitlin's hand.

"Okay." He turned and led them out of the house.

Chapter Twenty-five

For a while, no one spoke. Caitlin watched the trees go by, cloaked in a soft pearly mist. Magpies warbled, their calls mournful and jarring. Her head rested on the back of the seat as the car crackled over uneven bitumen. She'd never felt so tired, yet her eyes refused to close. The horror of the night was over but it was as if her body sensed there was still a long way to go.

"What do we tell the police?"

Micky was the first to answer. "I'm the only one that's broken the law. I'm ready to admit that I held Felix at the house and tried to make him talk. I'll tell them I gave Jace a key, but didn't know you were coming this weekend."

"You don't have to cover for me." Jace slowed the car and made the turn onto Forest Highway. "It's my fault Eli and Caitlin ended up at your house. I'm not going to try and weasel my way out of it." When he was angry, Jace sounded a lot like his brother. Caitlin wondered why she'd never noticed it before.

"I'm not covering for you." Micky turned in the front seat, she watched his face in profile. He looked tired, maybe as tired as she felt. "I'm trying to keep things simple. Uncomplicated. None of you were doing anything wrong. You just showed up at the wrong time." He turned to face her. "I'll tell them I invited Felix to the house, offered him money to tell me where he left Am—my sister." He turned away so she couldn't see his face. "I'll say Felix brought the handgun with him. As long as we don't mention the shotgun…" He trailed off.

"You mean if they don't know you had the guns, you'll get a lighter sentence?" The reality of the situation sunk in. Eli was dead and Micky would be going to prison. Caitlin finally managed to close her eyes.

When she opened them again, the sun was shining. The even hiss of tyres over a new, tarmacked road told her they were getting close to Mandurah. She caught Jace's stare in the rear-view mirror. His eyes were red-rimmed, unreadable. It occurred to her that without Eli, there was nothing left to connect them. The thought left her numb, as if her body had somehow purged itself of all emotion.

* * *

They waited on green plastic chairs, bolted to the floor. Micky stared blankly at the small television screen fastened to the wall in the corner of the room. An elderly couple sat to his left, the man pressed a blood-soaked dressing to his forearm. Occasionally, the door to the treatment area would swing open, spilling a tumult of voices and movement into the sparsely populated waiting room. The police would be arriving shortly, there'd be questions to answer, explanations to give.

It had been twenty minutes since Caitlin was taken away for treatment. Micky thought of getting up and going outside, breathing in the fresh morning air but the need to know how she was doing kept him glued to the chair. Besides, Jace was in no condition to take in information. He'd barely spoken in the car and now seemed intent on staring at the palms of his hands. It was shock, Micky had seen it before. Once the battle was over, it was the quiet moments that hurt the most. Too much time to think.

"How am I going to tell Mum and Dad?" Jace sounded confused as if the thought had just occurred to him.

The doors to the treatment area flapped open. A woman wearing dark blue scrubs strode out. "Mr Frost?" She looked around the small group of anxious faces. "Frost?" She whittled the name down as if running out of time and patience.

Micky elbowed Jace in the bicep, noticing how the man jumped at his touch. "That's you, isn't it?"

Jace looked up, eyes wide, his hair plastered to his head with sweat. He stood and walked towards the woman, head down as if he were in high school and had been summoned to the principal's office. Micky followed and they were both led through the swinging doors to a small room furnished with a coffee table and four chairs.

"I'm Dr Ashbourne." She looked from Jace to Micky. You're Caitlin's... um, is it husband?" She had grey eyebrows, thin and drawn together as if perpetually disapproving.

Micky noticed Jace's wince, but he made no move to correct her mistake.

"This is Caitlin's brother-in-law." Micky jerked his thumb in Jace's direction. "I'm a friend. How's she doing?"

She gave a curt nod and focused her attention on Jace. "Your sister-in-law will need surgery on her finger. The bone is splintered, she'll most likely need to be fitted with a partial cast. She's lost quite a bit of blood but not enough to require a transfusion. We've stitched the laceration on her ear." She paused waiting for Jace to respond. When he remained silent, she looked to Micky. "There's a bite on her calf. Caitlin believes it's from a spider. Do you know what sort of spider might have bitten her?"

It was the first Micky had heard of a spider bite. The surprise must have shown on his face. "Dr...um?"

"Dr Ashbourne." The woman's eyes were brown, dark and under the querulous browns seemed razor sharp. Caitlin had been attacked, they'd told the desk clerk as much when they arrived. It was clear the doctor found her injuries suspicious to say the least.

"You know Caitlin was attacked." Ashbourne's face was unreadable so he continued, "She was spending the weekend at my holiday house with her husband and brother-in-law. I know she spent some time hiding in the attic. That could have been when she was bitten. There's no shortage of spiders up there. Mostly huntsman and redbacks."

"I see." Ashbourne let out a long sigh. It was a tired sound. "We'll keep her in for observation. Monitor the bite. All going well, she'll most likely be released tomorrow or Monday."

"Can I see her?" It was the first time Jace had spoken since the doctor appeared. "Can I see Caitlin?"

Ashbourne regarded him with a stringent stare. "She's going down to theatre soon, but a short visit won't hurt." She nodded to Micky. "I'll take you both through."

"No." It came out too fast—abrupt. If he saw her now, he wouldn't be able to leave her. Micky gave the doctor what he hoped was an apologetic look. "Jace should go on his own. I'll hang around in the waiting room." He wanted to see Caitlin, make sure she was okay. Part of him almost needed to see her again. That was the problem. It would be better, he decided, if he backed off. What she needed now was family, not him.

Outside Accident and Emergency, the morning sun filtered through the carefully landscaped edges of a dull bitumen parking lot. Micky could feel the heat building in the cloudless sky. His mother would be awake, he glanced west towards the oncology wing. Less than twenty-four hours ago, he'd visited her. Leaving Felix alone in the cellar had been a risk. As it turned out, a costly one. He wished he could give her the news she'd been waiting fifteen years to hear—we found Amy.

Micky walked towards a small garden area with a set of concrete benches. He felt weary, like his bones were filled with lead. There wasn't much shade but it was nice to breathe clean air. The sharp smell of cleaning products that filled the hospital conjured up images of his mother, skin sallow and arms like sticks.

He noticed a police car pull into the parking lot. Two uniformed officers stepped out, their pale blue uniformed shirts reminded him of his years in the military. Micky watched them walk towards Accident and Emergency. They were younger than he'd expected. The older of the two couldn't be more than thirty. The sliding doors opened and the two men disappeared inside.

They were here for him, of that he had no doubt. Before the day was out, he'd be charged with a string of serious crimes. Rather than dread, he felt relieved. Not to be losing his freedom, but because it was finally over. He'd been at war with the world for so long, it would be nice to surrender. Peaceful.

There was a no smoking sign on one of the benches. Micky took the packet out of his pocket and lit up. The rich tobacco taste filled his mouth and slipped downwards into his lungs. *This is the last one, promise.* He spoke to Amy as he sometimes did. Only, for the first time, his thoughts were light, conversational as if she were sitting next to him smiling in that cheeky carefree way she had the last time he saw her.

He finished the cigarette, smoking it down to the filter. When he was done, Micky dropped it, crushing it under his boot. Before walking away, he picked up the flattened butt and dropped it in the rubbish bin at the edge of the small garden. The weariness had lifted. He crossed the parking lot and entered the Accident and Emergency Department.

Chapter Twenty-six

Caitlin pushed open the front door. Over the past five months, she had become accustomed to the hush of an empty house. Far from finding it lonely or depressing, she'd come to look forward to the serenity, the lack of noise or tension. She walked through the narrow entrance balancing a bag of groceries and her oversized tote, one in either arm, topped off with a few pieces of mail wedged under her chin.

Her wet shoes left a sloppy trail of prints through the house. She thought about getting the mop out and wiping up the mess, but decided there was no rush. She dumped everything on the kitchen table and struggled out of her damp coat. The rain hadn't stopped since lunchtime, coming down in urgent sheets, sharp and chilled. Her fingers were numb, almost blue with the cold.

As always, the sight of her missing digit took her by surprise. It was as if she expected it to reappear one day and couldn't help being disappointed when the oddly shaped nub remained. She rubbed her hands together and started unloading the groceries. A small tub of salad and a quarter of cooked chicken—dinner for one. *Now all I need is a cat. Make that ten cats.* Chuckling to herself, Caitlin hurried upstairs to run a bath.

She lay back enjoying the feel of hot water against her skin and the scent of the honey and jasmine bath bomb as it wafted in the air. It had been a brutal day. One she'd been dreading for months, but now it was over, there was light at the end of the tunnel. There was loneliness, but not without hope. Even the deep gouge on her calf ached less than usual.

She poured liquid soap onto a sponge and massage the scar. They never did work out what sort of spider bit her, but the infection that followed ate away at the surrounding flesh forcing the doctors to cut away the infected area. The puckered dip in her leg was ugly, like so much of what happened that night. That's how she'd come to think of the horrific events that made her a widow and left her scarred for life. *That night.* It was easier to have a name for it, at least it made discussing it easier. *Yes, I remember that night. No, I don't want to talk about that night.* She closed her eyes.

The water began to cool and her skin to pucker. The thought of standing and drying herself seemed like a tremendous effort. She wished she'd thought to put the heater on downstairs.

The shrill of the buzzer startled her. Caitlin sat up in the tub and reached for a towel. Hunched over, shivering, she rubbed herself dry before flinging on a fleecy robe and rushing for the stairs. She was halfway down when the buzzer bleated out another urgent demand. The rain had stopped, the incessant drum now dwindled to irregular drips as the gutters struggled with the overflow. She clutched the robe closed and approached the door.

A figure, large and dark outlined in the glass panel. She slipped the chain across the door and swallowed before squaring her shoulders. It was no good telling herself she had nothing to fear. She of all people knew that to be a lie. There was plenty to fear, things beyond her control. But living in fear was something she did have control over.

Caitlin opened the door to find Jace, blond hair clinging to his head in damp clumps, leaning against the doorframe.

"Jace." She couldn't help being surprised. It had been months since he'd last dropped by and then it was only a quick, painful meeting to discuss Eli's funeral.

"Hi. Can I come in?"

"Yes. Yes, of course." She stepped aside and let him enter. "Do you want coffee or... How about something to eat?"

He stood in the hallway, his broad frame filling the small space. "A glass of water."

"Okay. Come through to the kitchen." They performed an awkward shuffling of positions. He smelled like winter nights, damp with a hint of wood smoke. It occurred to her that he was taking great care not to touch her, but she dismissed the thought. She told herself that with Eli gone, they were bound to feel a bit awkward around each other.

Jace took a seat at the table while Caitlin grabbed a glass and filled it with chilled water from the fridge. "Wow. It's been raining most of the day. I can't believe the change in the weather. My hands were freezing when I got home..." She knew she was babbling, trying to fill the silence with inane chatter.

After placing the glass in front of him, she moved around the table and sat opposite him. "Your hair is wet. Do you want a towel?" She was half out of her seat when he stopped her.

"No." His tone was harsh. It made her think of Eli. "I'm fine." He picked the glass up and took a swallow.

She sat back and put her hands in her lap. She'd known him long enough to be able to tell when there was something on his mind. It had to be about Micky. About what happened today. "I know I haven't been around much lately–"

Caitlin felt a rush of relief, something in the way he looked at her when she opened the door set off alarm bells, but all she'd seen was guilt. "You don't have to explain, Jace. It's been... Well a strange time for all of us... After that night." There it was again. Everything always came back to those dark hours. "Strange for both of us. You needed time to grieve, I understand."

He nodded and picked up the glass, not drinking, just holding it. "Yeah. But now it's over. We can put it all behind us."

She'd been so focused on her own healing and what the future might hold, she hadn't given Jace much thought. Telling herself that his parents would take care of him and all the while secretly relieved that she didn't have to see his pain. Pain that would remind her she was supposed to be in mourning.

Caitlin reached across the table and let her hand rest on Jace's arm. "I hope we can."

Jace's face softened and for an instant he was the old Jace; easy going and sunny. He put the glass down and placed his hand over hers, clamping it in place against his forearm. "You know how I feel, Cat." He squeezed her hand, pressing her palm against his skin. "Eli's gone, but we're still here. We can be happy together. I can *make* you happy."

Caitlin pulled her hand away unable to believe what he was saying, but the words kept tumbling out. "I could always make you laugh, remember?" He reached across the table, but Caitlin dropped her hands into her lap. "It's okay. I'll square things with my parents, no one is going to judge us we–"

"Stop." The force of the word seemed to take all her strength. "Please, just stop." Her mind was reeling. All this time she'd thought Jace was her friend. The brother she'd never had. She laughed with him, trusted him, never realising he'd been waiting for an opportunity to swoop in and… She didn't want to think about what he hoped would happen.

"You don't have to feel guilty. It's over now… I don't know if you heard." He was looking in her direction, but not meeting her eyes. Choosing to let his focus rest somewhere over her right shoulder. "Micky was sentenced today." He waited for her to answer, finally meeting her gaze.

He seemed to want her to say something, just what, Caitlin wasn't sure. "I know. I was there." He flinched and she felt a quiver of uncertainty, a measure of guilt she hadn't expected to experience. "I'm sorry. I wasn't trying to hide anything. I just… There's no easy way to explain it."

"Explain what? What are you trying to tell me?"

Caitlin felt her fingers curling into fists. She forced herself to place her hands on the table. She noticed Jace's gaze flicker from her face to her left hand. The urge to cover the ugly stump came and went.

"I've been seeing Micky." The words were out and suddenly she became aware of her own voice. She'd rehearsed this moment in her head many times. No matter how much she prepared herself, the look of hurt in his eyes rocked her resolve. Only he wasn't hurt for his brother as she'd expected, he was angry because she didn't love *him*.

Water dripped against the window sill, the regular beat filled the silence. Caitlin pushed on, determined to finish. "It wasn't something we planned. It just happened." The words sounded so much like a cliché, she almost laughed. "I mean… Eli and I were having problems long before–"

"Before he was murdered?" He pushed his chair back and stood so suddenly that Caitlin shrank back in her seat. Jace gave a bitter sounding laugh. "What? You actually think I'm going to hurt you?" He turned away and stood facing the window.

"No. No. Jace, I didn't think that. You just seem so upset." She tried to explain herself. "I wasn't expecting… Well, the things you said. I know this must be a bit of a shock." She watched his back for some sign that he was listening, at least trying to understand. He remained silent so she pushed on. "I'm not doing this to hurt you, you have to understand. Micky and I… It's different. Easy. I know it's crazy, but I always felt like I was trying so hard to make Eli happy." She shook her head. "It never seemed to be enough."

Caitlin pressed her hand to her chest, steadying herself before continuing, "With good behaviour, Micky will be out in eighteen months. We're going to take it slow." Just thinking about a future with Micky made her pulse quicken. "Whatever feelings you have for me can't –"

"I heard you." His voice was throaty as if coming from somewhere deep in his chest. He kept his back turned. "That night in Blyte's house. I heard you."

Caitlin tried to make sense of what he was saying. She'd shut out so much of that night, details were a blur. The lines between what really happened and the feverish dreams she'd experience in hospital wound together so tightly, it was hard to recognise real memories.

"Heard what?" Even as she asked, a memory swam to the surface, poking its head into her conscious like something unnatural, a dreadful creature from the deepest ocean.

He turned and faced her. "He asked you to choose who got to live."

Caitlin wished she could cover her ears, but it was too late. She couldn't wipe the memory from her mind or the anger and pain off Jace's face.

"Jace." She gripped the edge of the table. "Please. I don't want to think about what happened." Suddenly the room seemed too small for the two of them. The air was stale and dry in her mouth. She wanted him to stop talking, leave and never come back. Seeing him reminded her of a half-forgotten version of herself. Someone she didn't want to be anymore. "There's nothing to be gained by going over things we can't change." She could hear her voice rising.

"You were screaming." His usually sunny-blue eyes were dark, threaded with red veins as if he'd been drinking too much and not sleeping. "I ran for the back door." He gave another humourless laugh. "I was desperate to get to you, save you. Protect you from Felix. I would have run in front of a bullet." He held up his arms and stepped forward. "That's the funny part, because you chose Micky. Felix asked you who gets to live and you chose him. My brother wasn't even cold and you were moving on." He dropped his arms, hands slapping against his legs. "I heard the words coming out of your mouth and I couldn't believe I'd spent so many years—"

"That's enough." She slammed her hand on the table. "You're not angry because I'm moving on from Eli." Jace took a step back. "You're mad because I don't want to be with you." As the words came out, everything began to make sense. The lengths Jace had gone to get her and Eli to go away with him for the weekend. The way he sided with her against his own brother. Caitlin felt herself cringe at the betrayal.

She pushed away from the table and stood. "I'm sorry I said what I did. I can't explain it. I won't try." Her voice sounded stronger. Maybe stronger than it had ever been. "I don't want to hurt you. But none of us are without guilt. We all played a part in what happened that night and now we have to live with it."

Jace's eyes were brimming with tears. "This is how you live with it?" His voice was low, almost a growl. "By letting the man that got Eli killed crawl into your bed?"

"You're the one that put us in that house." She heard her own voice rising, it sounded bitter and hard, as if coming from a stranger. "All this time I thought you did it out of kindness. I believed you were trying to help Eli and

I fix our marriage." She shook her head and stepped around the table. Jace winced as if her words were blows pelting him like fists. "You're the one that got Eli killed, not Micky. You." She held up her mutilated hand. "Look." Jace grimaced and tried to look away. "I live with the scars *and* the memories, I won't apologise for moving on with my life. For trying to find happiness."

"Cat, please."

"Don't call me that." She straightened her back. "I think you should go." Part of her wanted to wrap her arms around him. Beg for his forgiveness. Say anything so they could go back to how things used to be between them. But another, deeper fragment, knew they could never go back because whatever had existed between them was an illusion. That part of her life died one night, five months ago.

Jace swiped at his eyes with the balls of his hands. He opened his mouth to speak. She braced herself for his anger, but instead he turned and walked out of the kitchen. She heard his footsteps, heavy and swift in the hallway. The front door opened then clanked back into its lock.

Caitlin sat down and stared at the half empty glass of water left unfinished on the table. All she felt for Jace was pity. He'd lost his brother, and whatever misguided hopes he'd had for a future with her were smashed. She'd cared for him, loved him in a way. So much unhappiness, so much loss.

The rain started again, softer now, more like a gentle shower than the angry deluge of earlier that evening. Her thoughts turned to Micky. He'd most likely be in a cell, staring at blank walls. She wrapped her arms around herself wishing he was with her now, imagining what it would be like to listen to the rain together.

The next eighteen months would be hard. For Micky, the time would be almost unbearable, especially so soon after the loss of his mother. The thought of him stoically enduring his sentence pulled at her soul trying to drag her downwards like the rushing waters of the runnel at the back of Micky's house.

Caitlin ran her fingers through her hair and stood. Too weary to be bothered changing into her pyjamas, she began preparing her meal. She wasn't hungry, but she would eat. She would get through tonight and so would Micky. They would get through every night until they were together again. It wouldn't be winter forever.

THE END

If you enjoyed this book, please let others know by leaving a quick review on Amazon. Also, if you spot anything untoward in the paperback, get in touch. We strive for the best quality and appreciate reader feedback.

editor@thebookfolks.com

www.thebookfolks.com

Also by Anna Willett:

BACKWOODS RIPPER
RETRIBUTION RIDGE
FORGOTTEN CRIMES
CRUELTY'S DAUGHTER
VENGEANCE BLIND
THE WOMAN BEHIND HER

SMALL TOWN NIGHTMARE
COLD VALLEY NIGHTMARE
SAVAGE BAY NIGHTMARE

Made in the USA
Monee, IL
08 April 2020